The Superspy and the Great Feast

Eddie Ayala

The characters and events portrayed in this book are fictitious. Any similarity to real persons, living or dead, cities, or landscapes is coincidental and not intended by the author.

No part of this book may be reproduced or stored in a retrieval system or transmitted in any form or by any means, electronic, mechanical, photocopying, recording, or otherwise, without the express written permission of the publisher.

ISBN: 978-1-7320536-0-1
ISBN 13: 978-1-7320536-0-1 (paperback)
ISBN 13: 978-1-7320536-1-8 (e-book)

For you...my love

Contents

Prologue

The Black Hand

The stories surrounding the Black Hand are without origin. They have always been.

They speak of a great awakening from the depths of the earth—ancient and deadly, neither man nor beast but otherworldly, with an unquenchable appetite for death and destruction. Its hatred for mankind it makes known by mocking his governing institutions of goodwill, peace, and uniform order. It sentences the world to death, pledging an apocalypse unlike anything ever witnessed by humans, who can do nothing to stop its wave of destruction. Death will come to all. No man, woman, or child will be spared. In the end, it will reign over the earth under the banner of its own handprint that the strong will always vanquish the weak. And humans—those few remaining—will enter an eternity of servitude.

Of course, these are just stories, passed and reshaped over the years by runaway imagination. Evidence is lacking to support who or what the Black Hand truly is. All data thus far has pointed to an underground network of self-interest groups, still in the stages of infancy, proclaiming to be the Black Hand, and not some entity enraged with the world. Their mischievous ways are purposeless along with their aim for world domination.

Yet in the last few years, small-scale wars have erupted in different parts of the world for unclarified reasons. Nations have begun to arm themselves with nuclear weapons, threatening to do war with each other. And government institutions that have been in play for decades have collapsed overnight, replaced with extremists coupled by their ideologies. The world as we know it has suddenly become an unstable place to live in. It's almost as if an unseen shadow has emerged from out of nowhere and placed a dark spell upon the earth. Perhaps that *nowhere* is from the murky depths below, prepping the world stage for more wicked things to come.

If the Black Hand is real and the stories about it are also true, then there is no denying its commitment to total annihilation. The Black Hand will stop at nothing, absolutely nothing, to do away with the world that mankind has built and, in its place, establish its version of world order—even if that world order means the extinction of the human race.

Chapter 1

Anniversary

Desmond knew he was in a world of trouble when he heard the word *cozy*.

The real-estate agent didn't have a website or any pictures. He had vague descriptions instead. "The cabin was *cozy*," he said. It was cute, and it wasn't a cabin. It was a *cottage*, pronounced *ko-tash*. It was a *cute mountain ko-tash nestled beautifully within the awe-inspiring, majestic Willow Brook Mountains*—that was how he described it over the phone in a polished accent that almost sounded British.

Words like *cozy* and *cute* usually meant *cramped* and *ugly* in real-estate terms. Real-estate agents were known to view the world under a different lens that exaggerated proportions and brought out the vibrancy in the color green. The kitchen? *Economical.* The bathroom?

Comfortable. The bedroom? *Spacious.* The living room? *Lived in.* And the price? *Affordable.*

So as Desmond drove up to 916 Fir Tree Lane, he came upon an ugly, overpriced, small cabin in the woods, smothered by low-hanging trees, spider webs, and dry leaves, with a cramped living room, small bathroom, even smaller kitchen, and a bedroom big enough to fit a bed and only a bed, minus any wiggle room.

He laughed. He couldn't help it. He knew better than to act surprised, so he laughed even more. Aliana, on the other hand, was beaming with excitement and raced through the four-hundred-square-foot enclosure like a child through a toy store. It was hers. All hers. The mountains, the trees, the cabin, the stars, *everything*—hers for seven days.

Theirs was a fast-paced life of long working hours and no sleep, with very little time for each other. Their demanding schedules had finally brought them to their breaking points, channeling their rage and frustrations at each other, and not at work. It didn't take much to send the couple over the edge. A call, a text, a word, a glance, a sneeze, or even the sound of a high-pitched fart would have them at each other's throats, dinging the start to the night's main event featuring the five-foot-ten, 180-pound Desmond Williams against the five-foot, average-built, 120-pound Aliana May. The last few matches ended in a draw, and with their relationship still on the line, both felt the next would be their last. But their last never came. July 19 came instead. The date marked the commencement of their long-awaited and much-needed vacation, putting a temporary hold on all upcoming matches with the hope that it would also put a permanent end to their fighting careers.

Gone were cell phones, text messages, computers, and e-mails. *Gone* were six to seven-day workweeks, long working hours, and nonexistent sleep. *Gone* were high-rise buildings, streetlights, and bustling cars. Taking their place were pine trees, mountain streams, distant green hills, wildlife, glistening stars, moonlit nights, and the soft, gentle mountain breeze that only the natural world could provide. They were free. *Free* to forget their bustling lives back home. *Free* to reset and enjoy life without so much as a deadline to worry about. *Free* to think clearly again about the things that mattered most, and what mattered most was each other. It was going to be the fun-filled romantic undertaking they had promised each other six months ago, from hiking and picnics by the lake to dancing and candlelit dinners by night. They were going to enjoy every minute of it without so much as a moment to spare.

Monday, they slept all day. Tuesday, they slept half the day and spent the other half drooling and grunting mindlessly over television. One grunt meant to turn up the volume, two to change the channel, and three to pass the popcorn. By midday, they had evolved to burping as a more advanced form of communication. Farting by night. Wednesday, their bodies successfully managed to shed off their PJs and mutate into more casual wares. The hike they'd promised each other was long overdue, so they hiked: through the mountainous bedroom covers, past the narrowing and nail-biting bathroom passageway, into the cavernous comforts of the cramped living room, till finally reaching the safety of the couch. They were tired. At first, they panicked when they couldn't find the TV's remote control, but when they spotted a glimmer of plastic hope between the couch cushions, they breathed a sigh of relief and took in the grand fifty-inch panoramic spectacle of high-definition reality television. Thursday, they were feeling adventurous. They hopped into their four-wheel drive and set out to try the local mountain cuisine that Willow Brook was known for. By day's end, they still weren't quite sure what they'd eaten, only that it was the *Willow Brook Mountain special* of the day. They went to bed trying not to think about it despite the throbbing pain and excessive farting that came from their stomachs. By Friday morning, they found themselves dashing into the woods after their bouts with chunky diarrhea plugged up the toilet. While in their haste to expel poop, they basked in the natural mountain setting they had longed to see all week, admiring the sights even longer while in between squatting thrusts. It was excruciatingly beautiful.

Saturday marked their two-year anniversary. It was the one day they had talked religiously about for six months, and they were still unsure how they wanted to spend it. It had to be uninterrupted. That was their first requirement. Fortunately, Willow Brook had met most of that requirement. *Away from it all* was the official mountain slogan. At five thousand feet in elevation, that put them with little to no cell-phone reception, translating into no incoming or outgoing phone calls. There was also no Internet accessibility, meaning that Desmond couldn't amuse himself with his eighteen-and-over downloadable distractions. With the television unplugged, the first part of their plan was checked off. The second part, however, involved romance. Lots and lots of romance. Saturday had to be romantic. Their two-year anniversary demanded it. At first, they had set their hearts on candlelit dinner followed by dancing under the moonlight. But the idea came to a squirting end from the previous day's diarrhea-and-wilderness experience. The couple wasn't eager to try more local mountain cuisine.

"I'm not worried. The mountain will tell us what to do," Aliana said, so sure of herself.

"So far, it's told us to eat, sleep, watch TV, and it gave us diarrhea," Desmond responded nonchalantly. "I don't think we should be listening to the mountain anymore."

"Tomorrow will be different. You'll see." She smiled at him affectionately. It was the same smile he had fallen in love with two years ago.

Aliana was a real beauty. She had green eyes, framed by curly shoulder-length brown hair, with fair, light skin. Petite as she was, she was a force to be reckoned with. She stood her ground on issues of adversity and refused to back down when push came to shove. But moments of hardship were few and rare in her life. Aliana spent most of her time playing the role of the sweet thirty-something-year-old gal.

Desmond didn't quite give off the same sweet vibe. He towered over his girlfriend with a set of dark eyes, black hair, and a slight yet muscular build. People could never get past Desmond's looks. They couldn't see him as the successful thirty-one-year-old banker that he was or entertain the idea that he was an intelligent, methodical man. No. What people saw was the street thug or the athlete with the young, attractive white female. He could never get past the stares. The sight of them together always struck the same disagreeable chord among the crowds no matter where they went.

Aliana didn't care. She gave off hugs and kisses regardless of who was watching. She loved him, and he loved her. That was all that mattered.

The mountain woke them up early Saturday morning with sunlight that peeked through their bedroom window, resting gently on their faces. They got up, got dressed, ate a small breakfast, packed a lunch, and went out for a drive. The mountain led them through miles of meandering roads surrounded by green treetops that gave open to a beautiful azure sky. It took them around Willow Brook Lake, where the couple pulled over excitedly to enjoy a picnic lunch. Afterward, they walked hand in hand around the blue, sparkling lake when Desmond realized how funny it would be to throw Aliana into the water. He scooped her off the ground and held her over the edge.

"No. Put me down," she laughed in protest, kicking and screaming.

After a suspenseful minute, Desmond set her back down gingerly. As soon as her feet touched the grass and his arms pulled away from her waist, Aliana spun around and pushed him with all her might. Desmond fell backward into the lake, swallowed up in one big gulp. When he popped back up, he found his girlfriend laughing, pointing at his soaked body from the safe distance of the water's edge. He waded through the water quickly and reached out for her wrist.

"No!" she screamed, but it wouldn't work this time. Aliana fell face first into the lake. She popped back up, shivering, with a mouth full of water. She turned to her boyfriend with a set of stunned eyes ready to attack and kill, but after a minute she burst into laughter. The two splashed water at each other like children in a kiddie pool.

By midafternoon, the mountain led the two wet lovebirds into town, where they pulled into its plaza of bustling little shops that offered everything from homemade ice cream to mountain specialty bric-a-bracs. To their surprise, and by sheer act of God, this Saturday happened to be the one day out of the month that the plaza hosted a farmers' market. The colorful array of tents and buzzing crowds sent Aliana into a frenzied state of joy.

"You see"—she turned to Desmond with a larger-than-life smile— "it's the mountain. It told us to come here. This is perfect." Without a minute to spare, she raced into the multitude of tents, shouting at her boyfriend from six feet away to "Come on, hurry up!" and leaving him with little choice but to chase after his awestruck, crazy girlfriend.

They spread out and tackled the market from opposite ends in search of ingredients for the perfect anniversary dinner. Their tactic, however, proved to be of little help. There was simply too much food to choose from. Every tent they visited left them unsure what they were looking for. Thankfully, for times like these, Desmond had devised a rule of threes. *One*, if it looked good, he bought it. *Two*, if it smelled good, he bought it. And *three*, if it tasted good, he bought it. On the opposite end of the buzzing crowds, Aliana was trusting the mountain to tell her what to buy. It told her to buy everything. An hour and ten grocery bags later, the couple drove back to the cabin and spent the evening crammed inside the small kitchen, preparing chicken parmesan with a side of romaine lettuce, accompanied by wine and candlelight. By nightfall, the natural gas-driven fireplace had been switched on. The flames danced beautifully upon command. They ate quietly, their knives and forks doing all the talking. Occasionally their eyes would meet, followed by an affection smile or laughter. When they finished their meal, they sat lovingly on the couch, lost in the hypnotic flames that melted all their worries away.

"I can't believe it's been two years," Aliana said softly, spellbound by the crackling wood from the fireplace. "Two whole years," she said again, treasuring the sound of those three words.

Desmond kissed her cheek, bringing her in closer, losing himself in her warmth. She nestled her check tenderly against his chest and wrapped her arm tightly around his waist.

"It seems like such a long time ago," she continued.

"Twenty-four months ago."

"Twenty-four months ago—incredible," she said, still lost in the moment. "I wonder what that translates to in weeks."

"One hundred and four weeks."

"One hundred and four weeks—amazing. I wonder what that translates to in days—"

"Seven hundred and thirty days."

Aliana felt a smile growing on her face. "Hours?" she asked.

"Seventeen thousand five hundred and twenty hours."

"Seconds?"

"Sixty-three million seventy-two thousand seconds."

"Microseconds?"

"Twenty trillion gazillion microseconds." Aliana burst into laughter and smacked Desmond across his chest. "What? You asked," Desmond said innocently. "That's how long we've been together." He laughed.

"You see, that's what I love about you," she said, sitting up. "Always making me laugh. Always making me smile."

There was her smile again—the one that Desmond fell in love with two years ago today. They stared into each other's eyes, longing after one another.

"Now do me," she said.

"OK. But we just ate. So I might start off a little sluggish, but I'm sure I'll end strong."

"No. Not that, you pervert. I meant *me*. Tell me what you love most about *me*."

"Oh. Well, *everything*," Desmond said with a voice so suave it could melt cheese. Aliana slapped him across the chest again, causing him to choke on the wine he was sipping on.

"'Everything' is too vague, cheater! Tell me what you love about me…in great detail."

Aliana waited impatiently while Desmond struggled to regain his breath. After a moment, he looked up at the ceiling and pursed his lips together in thought. His eyes darted back and forth, and just when he was about to say something, he stopped himself and stared back at the ceiling again. He did this about three more times, and it drove Aliana crazy with anticipation. He knew it would.

"Come on," she begged anxiously.

"OK, OK." He cleared his throat and sat up. "Here goes." He cleared his throat again.

Aliana sighed.

"What…I love…about…you…is—"

The table vibrated.

Aliana jumped. Desmond's eyes quickly fell on the yellow casing on top of the coffee table. The plastic phone case slid across the hard surface from the vibration.

"I thought we agreed no phones." Aliana stared at him accusingly.

"We did."

"Then what's that?"

Desmond turned back to the phone. "I…I didn't realize I brought it with me," he said, confused, unsure what to make of it.

"Don't."

"What?" Desmond asked.

"Don't."

"Don't what?"

"Don't you dare."

"Don't I dare *what*?"

"Don't even."

"What are you talking about?"

"Look at it."

"What?"

"Don't you dare look at that phone."

"I'm not."

"Yes, you are."

"No, I'm not."

"You're looking at it right now."

"No, I'm not." Desmond looked at the phone.

"You just looked at it!"

"That's 'cause you're tricking me into looking at it." He looked at it again.

"You looked at it again."

"Well…stop…telling me…not to look at it, and I won't."

The phone somehow seemed to vibrate even louder, pitting the two into a staring contest to see who would look away first. Beads of sweat trickled down Desmond's forehead. His eyes shook with anxiety. Aliana remained calm, collected, staring deeply into his eyes, into his soul. She was an unblinking, intimidating force.

The two remained perfectly still as the vibration grew louder and louder and *louder and louder and louder and*—

"What if it's important?" Desmond finally looked away.

"Then let your bank flunkies deal with it."

"If they're calling me this late, then they can't deal with it."

"I can't believe we're actually having this conversation. We're supposed to be celebrating."

"We are celebrating."

"No, we're not. We're arguing."

"I'm not arguing.

"Yes, we are."

"All I'm saying is that maybe I should pick it up."

"No!"

"I'm picking it up."

"No, you're not."

"I need to."

"You're not touching that phone!"

The phone stopped. Dancing shadows and the sound of crackling wood filled the now-quiet living room.

"You see? All gone," Aliana said calmly. "All that arguing for nothing."

Desmond stared at the silent phone. He couldn't dismiss it as easily as Aliana had. He'd left it back home. He clearly remembered setting it on the kitchen table before walking out the front door.

Aliana cleared her throat. She cleared it a second time when it failed to grab Desmond's attention the first time.

Desmond turned back to his girlfriend, who was smiling and batting her eyes at him.

"Now, you were saying? What you love about me is?"

It took a moment for Desmond to get back into love mode again. He shook off the phone and turned the charm back on, showcasing those pearly white's that he was known for. He'd often boast to Aliana that if they were any whiter, they would glow in the dark.

He took Aliana's hand, to which her eyes beamed with excitement. "What...I love...about you...is—"

The table vibrated.

Desmond let go of Aliana's hand and snatched the phone away before she had a chance to take it from him.

"Dez!"

"It's an important client," he said, looking at his phone.

"You're supposed to be on vacation celebrating your two-year anniversary with the love of your life and not thinking about work."

"I am—two minutes. I'll just be two minutes."

Aliana's eyes went from big, round, and beautiful green to small, narrow, and red with anger. They pierced through Desmond like a laser beam.

"Two minutes," he said with half his body outside the front door. "Love you." He blew a kiss. She didn't kiss back.

The mountain was unforgiving at night. Desmond's body was struck with that harsh reality the second he stepped foot into the freezing temperature. He hugged himself to generate a little body heat—even hopped up and down. But it was no use. His body was growing painfully still by the minute. The cold was unbearable. The only real option was to turn back and forget this phone business, except it wouldn't let him. He could feel it vibrating from within the palm of his hand. It had other plans in mind.

Desmond peeked through the window to check on Aliana one final time before immersing himself with work. That's when he noticed the tears. Aliana was staring deeply into the fireplace with sad, watery eyes. As soon as the flames lost their magic, she sniffed and wiped the tears away before picking up the remote control and turning on the television.

Sorry, baby…had to…

Lying to her was never easy. It was an unfortunate task Desmond could never get used to no matter how much he tried. But it was an evil necessity. One he couldn't do without, especially on a night like tonight. Desmond had told no one where he was going. He'd gone so far as to make sure he wasn't being followed during their trek up north. To get a call this late, this high up, in an area where there should be no phone reception, from a phone he left back home meant only one thing. *They* knew where he was. They always *knew* where he was. His second-year anniversary would have to wait.

At least for now, he thought as he peered into the dark forest. Maybe a few days, a week, or even a month. He heard a twig snap in the distance. He turned and was met with darkness.

Maybe it would have to wait indefinitely.

Chapter 2

Operation Hidden Vault

Desmond pushed hard, but the mountain pushed back even harder. It forced him up hills, down valleys, and into parts no one would think of venturing in daylight, much less at night. His body gasped for air. His muscles tired and strained. The coldness that stung him earlier had been quickly replaced with heat and exhaustion. Whenever he stopped to regain his bearings, he could feel the warmth from his sweat trickle down his body, only to turn bitter cold. It was only a matter of time before Willow Brook's cold grasp would fully take hold of Desmond. He would need to quickly reenergize and make a decision which way to go next if he intended to survive the night.

Desmond consulted his phone. The coordinates and timer had decreased from the last time he checked.

Forty-five minutes until end of transmission.

Stressed, he looked up at the forest, finding himself dead center amid a dark maze of trees with branches so thick they choked away the blue moon, leaving the forest in ominous shadows, with multiple faux paths to nowhere. Desmond referred back to his phone as he panned around darkness. The coordinates decreased as soon as he faced a downward slope that led deeper into the trees. He sighed heavily. It was a known fact that the Agency never made things easy for their field agents. They set things up dangerously to see if they were still worthy of *the fight*, and there was nothing more dangerous and worth noticing than a man racing deeper into the dark woods, across the vastness of Willow Brook, a place known for high cliffs, deep pits, and caves, with dangerous wildlife roaming about. How ironic that such a majestic place that brought peacefulness by day could turn unforgiving, leaving one in abandoned despair at night.

Forty minutes until end of transmission.

Desmond took a deep breath and raced into awaiting darkness, guided only by the small hint of light coming from his phone. He felt the cold air rush past him. He felt branches nipping at his skin, leaving behind warm red streaks. He felt the ground shift from high to low, causing him to nearly stumble. Occasional blue highlights from the moon provided some scattered guidance. But they weren't enough. Desmond was still racing through the unknown, fighting the forest with sheer breath and might; all the while, he felt his mind drifting slowly away, away from darkness—away from the thick trees and scattered shadows, returning to the cabin and to the unforgiving image of Aliana, sitting alone on the couch in tears.

He loved her. There was no doubt. But did she know? Did she truly know?

***

Four years ago, the Agency had hit pay dirt when intel revealed that the Bank of New Mexico formed part of the elusive web the Black Hand organization used to filter its money.

Orders had come in: *infiltrate the bank, and get a closer look at the process at work.*

At this time, Desmond had become a rising star in the Agency. All those years under the tutelage of one of the most respected spies had not gone unnoticed, resulting in a flawless, successful record that had earned him the nickname "Super," from which "the Superspy" had evolved, regardless if the mission involved the use of the spy network or not. He was handpicked for Operation Hidden Vault, and without a moment to spare, he secured a job in the bank's Maintenance Department as part of his low to high-profile strategy. The strategy, however, required some delicate finesse. Inquiring about immediate promotion could arouse suspicion. And carelessly showcasing his unique blend of talents could pit his coworkers against him, gaining unwanted attention. A more methodical approach was needed, one that would be met with support from the staff. So he moved considerately by striking up conversations with his fellow employees whenever the opportunity presented itself. His positive demeanor, Colgate smile, and selfless inquiries about everyone's day made them feel warm and fuzzy inside. He impressed all with his ability to learn quickly. He amazed them like a street magician with his aptitude for complex numbers and calculations that he could perform on a moment's whim, always ending with applause. After two months, the janitor mathematician extraordinaire with the pearly white smile that everybody had come to grow fond of was promoted to bank teller. Six months later, the rising bank superstar who used to mop floors and empty everybody's wastebaskets became a loan consultant. Bank manager the following year, much to everyone's surprise, and much to the liking of the Agency. Desmond was finally in prime position to glance over the Black Hand's intricate web of numbers without so much as a blowback to his cover.

Financial reports revealed large sums of money coming from a myriad of ventures. The minute they streamed into the Bank of New Mexico, they were quickly broken up into smaller fragments to be fully vested into multiple markets and real estate. Nothing new or out of the ordinary. He wasn't impressed. The Black Hand network was not original. All the Agency had to do was shut off the valve, and the money would stop flowing in. Doing so, however, meant losing the only vantage point they had over the Black Hand's finances: a vantage point the agency desperately needed and wasn't going to let go off.

Hacking the bank was also out of the question. Any suspicious tinkering would blow his cover. Tracing the money back to its primary source was proving more difficult than Desmond had imagined. With the networks in constant flux, there was no telling where the money had originated from.

Now this was more like it. Desmond was impressed. The Black Hand's network had thought things through after all. A more tactful move was needed. What that next move was stumped him for months till it finally dawned on him. It was an obvious question he had overlooked, and he kicked himself for not thinking of it earlier.

"Who's making the decisions?" he asked himself.

The Black Hand was no financial genius—only a warlord. Someone else was behind this. The Agency had code-named this person *the Banker.*

Who was the Banker?

Desmond shifted his focus to the bank's inner circle. Someone within the membership had to be the Banker. He started with background checks and then took a more in-depth personal approach via luncheons, get-togethers, and weekend work functions. When that turned up nothing, he moved on to the bank's general manager, Luke. Standing six feet tall, with thick glasses and disheveled hair, the toothpick-shaped man had no business running the bank. Or any bank, for that matter. Luke had no prior bank experience or basic understanding of economics. His math skills were poor, and he lacked the social skills needed to interact with staff and customers. He stayed quiet most of the time, and when asked about financial matters by the upper echelon, he would turn to his bank manager, Desmond, to answer all their questions and then went about his daily routine of online gaming. Desmond wasn't sure how Luke had gotten the job. He played with the idea that it was a ruse by the Black Hand to ward off any suspicion of the bank, a plausible thought that unfortunately didn't take long to debunk when Luke couldn't make heads or tails over the monthly gains-and-losses report. Luke wasn't the Banker. Far from it. He was too clueless and mindless to understand how a bank functioned. Luke was a lost bet or an unfortunate kind gesture to someone, somewhere, who would not let the matter go.

Lastly came the ten-thousand-plus bank members. There was a high probability that someone within the mix was the Banker. This process of finding this someone entailed a close-up examination of every member's bank record with an emphasis on spending and investing trends. No one would raise any red flags if the bank manager decided to identify potential investors as a means to maximize lending profits. It was a move the bank liked and one that Luke couldn't fully comprehend. Unfortunately for Desmond, the process was tedious and slow. After three months, he had reached snapshot 138 with a little over 10,000 still pending. He was going nowhere. This process required years of hard work, a fact Desmond had carelessly underestimated. The mission would've continued this way had it not been for that one hot summer afternoon in May.

The air was arid and dry on that day, with dizzying heat. People trudged their way through the commercial plaza, sweating profusely through business attire that did not agree with the heat. Amid the sweltering herd emerged a short, pudgy man, wearing a three-piece business suit and what appeared to be a dark, wavy wig. There wasn't a bead of sweat on the man's face. He limped past the perspiring herd, and when he entered the air-conditioned bank, he didn't pause to absorb the coolness in the air like many had. Instead, he immediately went into Luke's office without so much as a knock on his door.

Luke removed his glasses, and the two immediately shook hands. Luke invited the man to sit across from him. He sat. They laughed. Signed documents. Talked for ten more minutes and shook hands again, and then the short, pudgy man exited the bank as quickly as he had walked in. The next day, large sums of money had been moved through multiple accounts.

On file, this man did not exist. There was no name, number, address, or date of birth to trace him back to a living heartbeat. He was a ghost. Desmond was tempted to inquire about the man but feared this might raise suspicion—or worse, put employees in harm's way. The Agency immediately responded by putting covert agents in the bank. They were ordered to open accounts and make daily deposits and withdrawals. If the Banker unexpectedly made a second appearance, they wanted to be there to quickly apprehend him. If for some reason agents weren't around, Desmond was given a code word to utter into his hidden collar microphone that would signal a full-on assault, leading to a quick extraction of the subject before anyone in the bank had a chance to soak in what had just happened.

Days went by. Nothing. Months passed. Still nothing. A year had come and gone with no sight of the Banker as the Black Hand's shadow loomed larger and stronger.

New orders came in: *flush out the Banker*.

This meant blowing his cover and doing away with three long years of investigative work. Patience was the key here, not recklessness. Desmond was so close to a capture. He argued his points, but the Agency wouldn't listen. They were growing desperate and willing to risk it all for a chance to stop the Black Hand network. Much to his dismay, Desmond moved forward with Operation Flushing Toilet. He went into the Black Hand's investments and tinkered with the numbers. If the Banker was watching, then it wouldn't take long for him to return. It didn't.

The Banker made his long-awaited return on a hot summer day in August much like the year before. He quickly rushed inside, sweating profusely, a far cry from the casual walk and demeanor Desmond witnessed a year ago. He immediately met with Luke, foregoing any handshakes. Luke quickly stood up and took off his glasses before the Banker shut the door behind him. Another unexpected move. The tinkering had obviously shaken up the short, pudgy man. Desmond could hear it in the man's voice. His muffled screams through the door were a bundle of nerves with poor old Luke at the receiving end, clueless about what was going on.

Wait!

It took Desmond a full minute to realize what had just happened. Looking over his left shoulder added more to the surprise. It was his office. It stood ten feet away. How strange. A second ago, he was watching the Banker make his overdue return from the comforts of his office chair. Now, suddenly, he stood in front of Luke's office door with his right hand wrapped so tightly around the handle that it turned his knuckles ghostly white. All Desmond had to do was open the door and put three long years of undercover work into action. Actually, three long years of *his* undercover work. It was Desmond Williams, the Superspy, the agent with the flawless record of accomplishments, who had realized the impossible task of locating one of the Black Hand's top-level operatives. Not the Agency or their flunkies. They may have stirred the hornet's nest by forcing Desmond to flush him out, and they may have provided the location where to flush him out to, but Desmond was taking all the risk. And with risk should go the reward. The capture of the Banker would be historic, possibly leading to the downfall of the Black Hand and its network. He would be heavily praised and go down in history as the best, if not *the* absolute best, agent in the Agency's saga.

Just turn the handle, and the celebration can begin.

Desmond tightened his grip around the brass knob till he heard his knuckles crack. With his other hand, he shut off his transmitter and tucked it back inside his collar. He turned his wrist and felt the door come loose. He pushed lightly against it.

"Are you the Banker?"

Desmond paused.

"I said, 'Are you the Banker?'"

That voice again, clearer this time.

"The lady at the window told me that I should speak with the bank manager. She pointed at you."

Desmond looked over his shoulder and caught a glimpse of the bank teller hiding beneath her counter like a scared child.

"I have a huge problem with the way you people do business here, and I'm not leaving until it gets fixed!" The voice was annoying. "Did you hear what I just said?" Very annoying. "I'm not leaving until you fix this!"

By now, the loud, obnoxious voice had captured the attention of everyone in the bank. Luke's door burst open unexpectedly. Desmond took a backward step, quickly releasing his grip on the handle. Luke stuck his head outside to see what the uproar was about. Behind him, the Banker was also curious, popping his head from behind Luke. Desmond turned away, and that's when he noticed the woman standing in front of him. He took hold of her arm. "This way, ma'am."

"Miss!"

"This way, miss," he corrected himself and lowered his head, careful not to be seen by the two men. He escorted her into his office.

"You're hurting my arm," she complained.

Desmond didn't care; he sat her across from him, keeping his eyes on Luke's office. Once he saw the door close, he breathed a sigh of relief.

"You people are amazing, you know that?" Her voice was full of sarcasm.

"What?"

"Unbelievable."

"What is?"

"You. You haven't listened to a single word I've said."

"I can assure you that I have."

"Then what did I say a minute ago?"

Desmond was about to answer when he stopped himself. She was right. Not a single word from her yapping mouth had registered inside his brain. Even as he escorted her into his office and she continued to roar into his ear about her problems, he heard nothing. The Banker had his full attention. Not her. Desmond tried to play it off by mumbling gibberish and smiling right afterward.

The woman laughed sarcastically. "I should've known better. You people are screw-ups. Real screw-ups. How do you sleep at night knowing that you're screwing people over? Huh? How?"

"Ma'am—"

"Miss!" she screamed.

"Miss." Desmond corrected himself again, grimacing. "I see you're frustrated. So why don't we start over. I'm sure whatever it is can be resolved."

"OK. Fine. I like that. I would like that very much. Let's start off with your full attention because I don't think I have it. You keep looking at someone behind me, and it's making me feel unimportant. I'm your customer. You should be focused squarely on me and not on someone else."

"I am focused on you."

"So look at me."

Desmond gave a small laugh. He'd finally had enough.

"I said, 'Look at me.'" She wasn't going to back down.

Desmond cleared his throat, fixed his tie, stood up, and prepared his right foot to kick her annoying ass out the front doors and into the middle of street during lunch-hour traffic. There was something far more important occurring ten feet away, and he didn't have time for this. He didn't have the time to stare deeply into her emerald-green eyes. Or to drool helplessly over her fair, light skin and curly brown hair. He didn't have time to gawk over her petite, slim figure, bound tightly by a gray business suit that accentuated her midsize breasts, which called out to him hypnotically by his first and last name.

"What...uh...what seems to be the problem, miss?" Desmond sat back down, buttoning up his coat, fixing his tie again.

"Just look at this. Right there, right freaking there." She showed Desmond her credit-card statement. It turned out she had been overcharged. "Honestly, is there even a brain among you? I can't understand how..."

While she raged on with insults, Desmond accessed her account and removed the overcharge. "Fixed."

The woman paused briefly. "What did you say?"

"It's fixed." Desmond stared deep into her eyes, lost in a pool of green.

"It's...fixed?"

"Yes. Fixed. Anything else I can help you with?"

"Uh...no."

Desmond returned her credit-card statement, which she took back rather slowly. She stood up, still confused by what had just happened. The rage she wore earlier had subsided to a calmer demeanor.

"That was…all I wanted," she said softly. "Usually it's a fight and a few days to get something like this done." She gave a half smile, which blossomed into a full-on beautiful smile. Desmond was in love.

"It was my pleasure, miss."

"Aliana."

"Aliana," Desmond repeated.

"Aliana May."

Desmond returned the smile and continued smiling the entire time he watched her leave. She was a real spitfire. Tough. Direct. All in all, he liked her, and he kept on smiling when a horrifying thought crept its way inside his brain. Quickly, he bolted out of the office, shoving customers out of the way. With one swift tackle, he slammed into Luke's office door, causing the bank manager to jump back and fall off his chair. Frantically, Desmond searched the room.

"What's going on?" Luke was visibly shaken. "Everything all right?"

Desmond's eyes fell on Luke's computer. He was busy playing his stupid games. Desmond rushed back out into the lobby and scanned the crowd. He was met with confused eyes, customers no doubt thinking him strange. As he searched the room, he felt his heart sinking deeper and deeper into his gut. The Banker was gone. To make matters worse, there wasn't a single field agent in sight. Of course, there wasn't an agent in sight. That's because Desmond Williams, the Superspy, the absolute best agent in the Agency, had taken it upon himself to disregard protocol and complete his mission solo, only to fail for the very first time. And not just fail but fail miserably.

Operation Flushing Toilet was a complete flush. The Agency withheld punishment while the matter was still under investigation and left Desmond stationed at the bank in case the Banker decided to make another return visit. But a third visit was highly unlikely. With the Black Hand's deposits decreasing by the day, there was very little hope of setting eyes on the short, pudgy man again. Whether or not the

Agency wanted to admit it, the bank was a form of punishment. It was Desmond's daily reminder of failure. He had single-handedly lost the only lead the Agency had ever had over the Black Hand. The loss proved unbearable at times, bringing bouts of depression. Desmond wondered if the Agency would ever trust him again with another mission.

Despite the fallout, there was a one small comfort. It came from a rather unusual source that had appointed herself as his only client. Aliana would frequent the bank and ask Desmond to assist her with her banking needs. Banking needs meant check deposits and account withdrawals—tasks anybody could do, but Aliana was convinced that only Desmond could do them correctly. She was annoying at first, but found her later to be an amusing and pleasant distraction from the gloomy reality surrounding him. Soon, deposits and withdrawals turned to financial advice.

"You're overdrawn again," he informed her on occasion.

"What do you think I should do?"

"Well." He clicked a few times on his computer. "Stop spending so much money on shoes and body wash. Let's start there."

"That's not possible. That's like asking me not to breathe."

Desmond laughed. She was one of the few people who had the ability to make him laugh. He also found her easy to talk to. There wasn't a single subject she wouldn't be excited to talk about even if she had no clue what the subject was. She was keen to his moods as well. Aliana could sense his bouts with depression and would go out of her way to cheer him up with a surprise lunch or a joke greeting card. Over time, their conversations went from financial dealings to what they did over the weekend. Weekly visits became daily visits, and luncheons turned into spontaneous after-work dinners. He enjoyed their time spent together, but like everything in Desmond's world, it wouldn't last for long.

The Agency apprehended Luke once the money dried up. They rested on the chance that he could provide some valuable insight into the Banker's whereabouts or possibly the Black Hand. They were quickly disappointed—not surprising to Desmond. Luke knew nothing. He was recruited from a homeless shelter by a group of strangers and promised a new life as long as he played the role of a bank figurehead and did absolutely nothing. The strangers would provide the staff needed to run the day-by-day operation. From time to time, someone would come in to make sure everything was running smoothly and make financial decisions. Whenever this person showed up, he was to remove his glasses immediately.

"Why?" the Agency asked.

"I'm blind without them. I only see fuzzy shapes," he answered.

Luke was an indirect victim of the Black Hand; his only real crime was seeking a change from a life that provided very little hope or future. He went to jail instead. The Agency's inquiries into the bank forced the feds to shut down the financial institution. Desmond was ordered to report to a hidden base in Pescadero and await further instructions. He never got a chance to say good-bye to Aliana.

***

Desmond came to an abrupt stop. The coordinates were coming from a cave dead ahead. He approached it cautiously; twigs snapping underneath his shoes did nothing to ease the tension he was already feeling. He held up his phone to shed some light into the cave's gaping mouth, but the tiny glow lacked the strength to penetrate the darkness within. As he drew closer, he anticipated a bear or a mountain lion charging out. But nothing came. He was relieved, although his relief was short lived when he stepped foot inside the cave and heard his steps echo deeper and deeper into the abysmal unknown. This wasn't over yet. There was still more lying in wait.

Ten minutes before end of transmission.

Chapter 3

The Message

His steps were careful and slow, kicking up dirt and rocks with the sound ricocheting off the walls to resonate deeper into the cave. The faint light from his phone scarcely made visible the low-hanging, jagged ceiling and sharp, extruding walls that encompassed the narrow passageway like a misshapen mouth coming forth out of the darkness. The mouth released a breath of cold air that caused Desmond's body to shiver uncontrollably. Another blast caused his teeth to chatter. He hugged himself tightly to keep the heat from escaping his body, but that seemed to make matters worse. The mountain trek had been unkind, leaving him spent and overcome with soreness. He was vulnerable to every sudden muscular move, and with the cave's unforgiving blasts, he responded physically, followed by unbearable pain. The sudden faint echoes of rushing water forced him to a complete stop, the sound of dirt crunching underneath his feet. The water was coming from down below. Desmond peered into a bottomless pit that lay only inches away from his boots. He consulted his phone one last time before it fizzled lifelessly in his hands.

Five minutes till end of transmission.

Desmond tossed the dead weight over the edge and watched it disappear down the throat of the pit. Transmissions were never the same. Some were more perilous than others, and not all agents were expected to make it. Those who made it proved themselves to be above the cut and were rewarded with the mission. Those who didn't were forgiven and lived to fight another day. He *could* forget it all and make his way back to the cabin and spend whatever remained of the evening with Aliana. No doubt she would like that very much—only he would have to explain where he'd disappeared off to. Everything would be forgiven. It always was. Yet, as pleasing as the thought was, Desmond could sense something down below. A dark and sinister presence loomed in the belly of the abyss. With the level of difficulty a transmission required came the importance of the mission itself. So far, this one had been no joke, leaving him completely drained.

The darkness called. It was time to answer. Forget it all and live to fight another day, or make transmission by risking everything and jumping into the unknown, possibly to his own death. In that moment, Desmond felt a surge of adrenaline course through his body, followed by a newfound power that rejuvenated his muscles. The Superspy within him came alive. He leapt into the air blindly, feeling his body in free fall, flailing against the rushing updraft of cold air.

Splash!

The current forced him downstream, making it difficult to keep his head above water. Desmond fought for breaths of air and kicked in the direction of the current, desperately trying to swim with and not against it. But the overpowering blows of rushing power proved too much, tossing him everywhere, leaving him disorientated. The undercurrent tugged at his legs once. Twice. Before he could act, it tugged a third time, taking him into the dark below, pinning him against the bedrock with an invisible grip that refused to let go. Desmond kicked and thrashed, but the grip squeezed like a rattlesnake, forcing the last bits of air out of his lungs until his body stopped thrashing, legs stopped kicking, and eyes became weary and closed. The world around him had grown quiet and still. His body drifted aimlessly in watery limbo once the grip realized it had won the struggle and let go. The cave was now his home; the water, his grave. He would float forever and ever in darkness till the waters stripped him bare of skin, muscle, and organs, fossilizing his skeletal remains into the watery deep.

Like a heartbeat it came—a shimmering speck of hope whose faint light reached Desmond's face from out of the darkness. It beckoned the life left in him to pry open his eyes and kick vigorously. With all his might, Desmond kicked. The grip reemerged and tried to retake control, but Desmond broke free, swimming toward the pulsating light, reaching out for its beating heart as it drew closer and closer. The grip took control of his legs, arms, chest, and neck. Desmond's fingers pierced through the water's surface as the grip squeezed his body fiercely when he was suddenly swept away by a sudden rush of cold air.

Desmond broke through the water's surface with a gaping mouth. His desperate lungs expanded rapidly from the sudden intake of air whose unbearable pressure came undone when a desperate call to life was made, mixed with an outpouring of water and thrashing coughs. Desmond rubbed the water away from his eyes as he tried to recenter his focus of where he was. He was nowhere. And so he swam desperately, trying to escape his watery keep, when it finally gave way to smooth rock, allowing him to crawl the rest of his way out. Desmond collapsed on his back, taking in deep breaths. His body was vexed with aches and pains. His head throbbed from the current's excessive blows. He moaned. The cave acknowledged his pain ten times over in an all-encompassing echo of mockery. After a moment, he sat up, clenching his teeth from the agony of overspent muscles. To his surprise, the shimmering hope that had championed his revival sat next to him. It was a beacon.

The pulsating light exposed a tiny rock island encircled by a sparkling blue lagoon. Limestone pillars supported the confined space with red-white stalactites hanging low from the ceiling like misaligned teeth. The cavern walls curved downward and cupped the lagoon into a small mound of paradise, only this slice of utopia came with a few comforts from home: a desk, chair, canned food, bottled water, blankets, dry clothes, and an exact duplicate of Desmond's phone. If that weren't strange enough, there was also a pair of glasses resting on top of the desk. It was the only item that seemed out of place since he didn't wear glasses—if that made any sense.

Every bone in Desmond's body cracked as he stood up. He staggered across the tiny island, planting both hands on the desk to help ease himself into the chair. The glasses piqued his curiosity. Even as he drank from the bottled water and dried himself off with towels, he never took his eyes off them. He picked up the pair, coughed, and examined them carefully. He looked through the lens, thinking he would see something hidden or out of the ordinary. Nothing. There was nothing unusual about their design. This only seem to add to the mystery of what they were intended for, other than the obvious choice of putting them—

Click!

A surge of electricity raced across his head. His newly discovered piece of paradise was transformed instantly before his eyes. A dome ceiling materialized from out of thin air. Ceiling lights followed and then offices, computers, and stairways. White marble flooring rolled out where the lagoon and rock island once stood. The cavern walls were now made of soundproof material that accentuated the ringing of telephones, keystrokes, and buzzing computer sounds accompanied by the pitter-patter of field agents hastily bouncing back and forth from one workstation to another. Desmond recognized this place. It was Central Command, and he was experiencing it through augmented reality, a technology the Agency had been experimenting with for years. The Agency's hope had always been to bring every field agent to Central Command for mission briefings regardless of where they were in the world. Augmented reality was that hope fully realized. A far better cry from video and tape-recorded transmissions or agents lurking in shadows with top-secret manila envelopes. Desmond was impressed. Everything felt real. Too real. In fact, Central Command was in complete disarray.

"Superspy." Desmond turned and saw Mark Stencil, Central Command's chief officer, stomping his way toward him. Stencil stood larger than life at six-foot-four and dwarfed just about anyone who stood beside him. At fifty-five, he was a heavyset behemoth who sported a thick mustache and buzzed haircut, with a signature belly that slapped away any poor fool that stood dangerously close. His voice was booming and commanding. There were rumors that when this man cried, laughed, or made love, he sounded the same: very loud and very booming.

"Thank heaven's balls you're here." Mark offered his hand.

Desmond shook it, surprised at how strong and real the grip felt. "It's been a long time, chief."

"Too long. Welcome back."

"Thanks." Desmond turned and took in the surrounding chaos of agents.

"Under normal circumstances, I'd ask you to sit and talk about old times," Stencil said, noticing the look of concern plastered all over Desmond's face.

"But this isn't normal."

"Far from it."

"Then what's going on?"

"Last night at exactly oh-five-hundred hours, redneck nuclear physicist Billy Bob Billy Jeff Jenkins escaped while en route to Black Portal detention center."

"What? How?" The news caught Desmond by surprise.

"Militia unknown," Stencil answered and looked up. Desmond followed his gaze to where footage from a soldier's helmet cam played out from a panoramic video screen that encircled the dome ceiling.

The soldier exited the vehicle and looked up to find dozens of black stealth planes with massive wingspans hovering over them against a starry night sky. The soldier, shadowed by several others who quickly jumped out of their SUV transports, opened fire. The stealth planes fired back with blinding spotlights. The footage became whitewashed and then blurry, and as it refocused, the soldier was caught in a firefight with several men in black military gear, rappelling down the stealth planes. The soldier was quickly apprehended at gunpoint and forced to watch a second group of black-clad men set up explosives against an armored vehicle's back door. The explosion blew the door apart. The men rushed in and extracted a man in handcuffs. As the soldier turned back to his captor, he found himself staring down the barrel of a gun. White light. End of footage.

"There were no survivors," Stencil said somberly.

The words weighed heavily on Desmond, who shook his head in despair. He knew some of those men. They were his friends.

"Superspy!" A sinister laugh echoed throughout Central Command. "I know you can hear me," the voice mocked.

Desmond raised his head slowly and looked up with determined eyes toward a smiling Billy Bob Billy Jeff Jenkins. His wild round red eyes, spiky blond hair, and freckled face gave off the image of a crazy redneck scientist.

"I know you're watching this," he said in his hillbilly redneck accent. "I'm sure your precious *Central Command* or *Command Central* or whatever the hell they like to call themselves pissed their trousers when they heard I flew the coop and fetched you out of the hole you like to sleep in. Thought you put me away for good, didn't you? Thought you could cage me up like an animal. Like a...like a ravenous possum whose only crime was wanting to cross the road onto new territory, to mate uncontrollably till he was apprehended and denied! You were wrong. *Dead wrong!*"

A graphic image of the United States materialized, with major metropolitan areas turning bright red. "Right now, I got every missile I own pointed at every one of your beloved cities. I plan to use them." He giggled. "You hear me, Superspy! I plan to use them all! Every shopping center, coffeehouse, mall, strip club, outhouse, all-you-can-eat Asian buffet, ninety-nine-cent store, and anything else you could think of and love...*gone!*" Missiles flew in simulation across the graphic image, finding their marks and blanketing the country with massive explosions, turning the video screen completely white.

"And if by some chance my carefully crafted PowerPoint illustration didn't make the point clear, then let me further clarify my point." The screen switched back to Billy Bob Billy Jeff Jenkins, holding a bucket of BBQ ribs. "I plan to do to your beloved country what I'm about to do to these mouthwatering, juicy ribs smothered in Agua Dulce BBQ sauce." He shoved ribs into his mouth, savoring each bite, licking his fingers clean, moaning at times.

By now, everyone in Central Command had stopped working to witness the sickening spectacle above their heads. Yes, it was displeasing to the eyes but delicious to the appetite. As a result, lips were licked, and stomachs growled, wanting BBQ for lunch.

The mad scientist swallowed the last of the ribs. He looked coldly into the camera and wiped his mouth with his white coat sleeve, smearing BBQ sauce all over his face so he resembled a savage cannibal. "You can't stop me this time. Nothing can stop me. Now, watch as your beloved country burns...*in four days*."

"Four days?" Desmond turned to Stencil, who shrugged.

"That's right—I said it. *Four days.* Bet you're wondering, *Why doesn't Billy Bob just push the big red button? Why doesn't Billy Bob Billy Jeff Jenkins just end it all?* Well, I can't! There's a comfort level to all this world domination, and I ain't comfortable!" The redneck scientist took a look around his domain and seemed dissatisfied with what he saw. In the background were soldiers still clad in heavy armor, vacuuming, sweeping, and wiping down windows. "Been a while since I've been in my secret lair. Hallways need rebuffing, toilets need scrubbing, and offices need vacuuming. I can't conquer the world in this mess. I also need to upgrade my computer monitors. I still got those old cathode-ray tube thick screens from the 1980s. I want to replace them all with those flashy flat-screen TVs everyone talks about. The ones that look cool when you hang them up on the wall. Know which ones I'm talking about? But after that"—his voice got serious again—"once everything's clean and updated…the world *burns!*"

The video switched off. Everyone in Central Command returned to chaos mode.

"Every field agent is on this mission, except for one." There was no doubt in Desmond's mind that the last part of Stencil's sentence was meant for him. Desmond looked past the thick mustache and directly into Stencil's watery eyes. *Impossible.* This man didn't cry. He was under orders not to.

"We need you," he finally added, a tear streaming down his cheek.

"You got me."

"Thank you, Superspy. As always, the world is in your debt." End of transmission.

The cave returned to normal. Desmond took off the glasses and tossed them back onto the desk. He found daylight creeping its way inside the cave from a small opening across the lagoon. He jumped into the clear blue water and swam toward it.

When he stepped foot outside the cave, he caught the sun rising over the distant mountains and took a moment to take in the view before he jogged back to the cabin. He wasn't sure what to tell Aliana.

He'd been gone the whole night when he was only supposed to be gone for two minutes. How was he going to smooth this one out? He wasn't sure. It was a recurring quandary he was confronted with each and every time he was on a mission. One that he would somehow manage to slide by, but one that she was growing tired of.

***

Nine months after Operation Flushing Toilet, his thoughts drifted back to the green-eyed brunette from New Mexico. He missed her smile. Her perfume. Her annoying laugh. And above all, he missed her company. Their luncheons and mindless conversations had the power to make him forget for one brief moment that a malevolent being was bent on conquering the free world. He'd often find himself wishing he could go back in time to enjoy those moments all over again.

The Agency had warned their field agents about personal attachments; they led to compromised focus and judgment. In short, they were dangerous. Desmond never felt compromised whenever he was around Aliana. He was fine, and his focus was dead on, like a laser beam. In fact, whenever he was with her, she made him feel unstoppable. He was worried about her. That's all. A lot could happen in nine months. He simply needed to know that she was OK and that her shoe and body wash spending had not gone uncontrolled. And…if she had met someone. His curiosities were all innocent, and what better way to satisfy them than to get behind the wheel of his car and endure a four-hour drive back to New Mexico on a Saturday night with no clue as to her whereabouts? Sure, he could have the Agency locate her, but he didn't want them to know.

As he drove back to New Mexico, he remembered how often *the bookstore* came up in their conversations.

When the world became too much to bear, the bookstore was always there.

It was her jingle; the bookstore, her place of solace. She enjoyed walking the aisles and randomly picking up books with interesting covers and with the potential to lead to an interesting read. She found comfort in sitting at the bookstore's coffee shop, sipping her espresso, watching people pass by. The chances of finding her at the bookstore on this particular night after a nine-month hiatus were slim to none. His chances went into the negative when he realized that all he had to go by was *the bookstore*. There were many bookstores in New Mexico. All with unique names. What were the chances that the one he was searching for was named the Bookstore? But lo and behold, there it was. The Bookstore! His odds had increased and were now in the positive. If by some godly miracle he found her inside, then it would be quick. A quick glimpse was all he needed—quick enough to see that she was all right. He promised himself he would leave right after. However, when he entered the bookstore, and his eyes landed on the corner table of the coffee shop, and he was met with the same smile and look of surprise, he looked longer than he promised himself he would. They hugged like old friends.

"Oh my God! I was wondering whatever happened to you," she said, her face beaming. "When they closed the bank, I thought I'd never see you again."

"I'm in Pescadero now. I work for corporate. They got me going everywhere," he lied.

"Pescadero—that's far."

"I know. Tell me about it." He laughed.

"What are the odds that you happen to wander into my bookstore so far away from home?"

Desmond grinned. He'd forgotten how sharp Aliana was.

"I take it they don't have bookstores in Pescadero?" she added with a smirk and a touch of raised eyebrows.

"No, they do," he said. "But they don't have what I am looking for." Desmond smiled.

"Well, in that case, I'm glad they didn't." Aliana smiled back.

They remained smiling at each other for such a long time that passersby thought they were creepy, smiling bookstore mannequins. That night both had made it obvious that neither wanted to be friends. Their romance quickly blossomed. Aliana moved in with Desmond, much to the dismay of the Agency. He was warned about his relationship. It was deemed unsafe. Desmond disagreed. The Agency argued that Aliana needed a normal life with someone who could provide her with the makings of such: a house, a family, a family dog, and above all, stability. The Superspy could not provide that, they told him. Desmond wouldn't listen. Much like they didn't listen to him during Operation Hidden Vault. He was returning the favor.

What was he fighting for? He'd ask himself year after year. When everything was said and done, and he rescued the world again and again from total annihilation, there was nothing waiting for him at home. No one to come home to. No one to smile at or with. *What was he fighting for?* One look at Aliana and the answer came quickly.

Because of this, the Agency had little confidence in the Superspy. He was called to active duty from time to time but was never given an important assignment. Just random cleanup missions. Desmond didn't mind. He preferred it that way. But as the missions became frequent, they turned into constant hurdles in his relationship with Aliana. Whenever he was called to active duty, he told her he was on corporate assignment to rescue a bank from going belly-up. While he was shooting it out with bad guys and facing death, she was at home thinking he was sitting behind a desk and inputting numbers.

With every assignment, the truth became more difficult to disguise, especially when he came home with injuries.

"What can I say? I love bike riding," he said one time when he came home with a black eye. "What can I say? I love mountain climbing. Helps me release stress," he said another time with a cast over his right arm. "What can I say? I love bull chasing," he said on a third occasion when he came home with a gunshot wound to his right buttocks and played it off like a bull's horn had pierced his ass.

With the Black Hand's shadow steadily growing, the calls were more frequent. There was nowhere he could go that kept the call from interfering. They came even while at her favorite bookstore. Desmond noticed how upset this made Aliana. His out-of-town trips were more common, leading to fights before and after. If he could only tell her the truth. But doing so meant revealing who he really was and what he did for a living. This would endanger her, and he loved her too much to put her in harm's way. He could never tell her about the ass whooping he gave bad guys or how many times he had saved the world from total nuclear meltdown.

She's safe not knowing any of this, he told himself each morning. That became the saving grace for his lies. She would only know him as Desmond Williams, the phony-baloney corporate banker, and not Superspy, badass extraordinaire. He tried to balance his guilt with gifts and exotic vacations that could never be fully appreciated. Each trip, he was called away. Each gift was opened after leaving for a mission. Aliana was always left to enjoy everything by her lonesome. Much like this vacation.

Desmond took a minute to gather his thoughts when he arrived back at the cabin. He still wasn't sure how he was going to explain himself. He reeked of murky water and was covered in dried mud, with a half-torn shirt and ripped jeans. After a minute, the only explanation that came to mind was that he'd run into Bigfoot in the middle of the woods and fought him all through the night. He sighed and opened the door slowly.

Aliana was asleep on the couch, still wearing the clothes from the night before. It was obvious to Desmond that she had passed out after waiting up for him most of the night—probably very worried. He sat next to her and brushed her hair back. That's when he noticed it. Her left hand. It dangled lifelessly off the side of the couch. Quickly, he pulled her up and pried open her eyes. They were lifeless. He pressed his head against her chest to listen for a heartbeat. It was faint.

Noise!

Desmond looked over his shoulder and found a dark shape glaring at him from the kitchen doorway. He stood up, grabbed the wineglass off the coffee table, and struck it against the table top until he was holding a makeshift shard.

The shadow raised its right hand. Desmond rushed forward, pinning it against the wall, holding the shard against its face while pressing down hard onto its neck with his left forearm, choking the life out.

"It was painless…it was painless," the shadow blurted out as he gasped for air. He was waving his Agency badge in front of Desmond's face, but the Superspy didn't care.

"Sa…io G…m…z," the shadow muttered.

"What?"

"Sabio…Gomez," he said in a gasping voice. "Yo…ur…partn…er."

"I don't have a partner." Desmond pressed harder into his neck, taking more of his air away.

"You…do…now." Sabio was on the verge of losing consciousness when Desmond finally let go. The man dropped to his knees, gasping for air.

Desmond knelt down next to Aliana to make sure she was all right.

"She went out looking for you." Sabio massaged his neck as he stood up. "She kept going deeper and deeper into the woods. What was I supposed to do?" He pulled out a stun gun from underneath his shirt that quickly caught Desmond's attention. He tossed it over to the Superspy, who caught it effortlessly. "She didn't feel a thing. She'll be out for four days…think this was all a weird dream."

Desmond examined the gun and then tossed it away, unimpressed. He carefully lifted Aliana off the couch and carried her into the bedroom, where he set her down gently onto the bed. He covered her up with the blanket and leaned down to her ear.

"Be back in four days. Love you." He kissed her forehead and left.

Chapter 4

Sabio Gomez

A beat-up silver cargo van bounced its way down the mountain road, leaving behind a wake of dust particles that sparkled against the rising morning sun, followed by the sound of heavy-metal music.

Sabio Gomez took to the winding roads like he would any video game: with a set of intense eyes and quick sips of his root beer. When the road shifted right, he gripped the steering wheel and steered right, feeling the weight of his body shift in the same direction. When the road turned left, he gripped the wheel and steered left, feeling gravity pull on his belly fat the same way.

What a fantastic video game. Bonus points for staying within the lane.

He took a sip of his root beer, smiling the whole time. Sabio never took anything seriously. At thirty years old, he was your class A computer geek and weapons specialist. Curly shoulder-length black hair, unshaven face, tight T-shirt that showed off his gelatinous upper frame, and worn-out, faded jeans with flip-flops to match his life slogan that life was about being completely relaxed at all times. As soon as the drum solo hit the speakers, Sabio raised the volume and tapped the dashboard relentlessly with his fingertips. He turned to Desmond for a little joint session love, but the Superspy sat quietly in the passenger seat, watching the scenery pass by. The man had not moved an inch since setting foot inside the van nor uttered a single word—not from the onslaught of drum solo beats or Sabio's annoying root beer sips.

Sabio lowered the volume and took another loud sip from his drink. He watched Desmond closely, unsure what to make of him.

"What?" Desmond asked, not taking his eyes off the window. It was obvious he was annoyed.

Sabio snickered. "I was wondering when you were going to say something." Sabio set his root beer down. "You were never this quiet."

"How would you know?"

"Oh, believe me, I know." He burped.

The two continued to remain quiet for a minute or two.

"You don't remember me, do you?" Sabio turned away from the road briefly, anxious to see what the Superspy was about to say.

"No."

"The Killer Butcher incident. The EMX satellite. They ring a bell?"

"You're confusing me with another agent." Desmond rubbed the sleep away from his eyes.

"No, I'm not. Trust me. I was there. Not physically, I mean, but I was there. I was one of your lifelines. You called me for tech wizardry. The one and only Sabio Gomez at your service." He said his name like a showman, waiting for a round of applause.

Desmond said nothing.

"*Really?* I hacked you into the EMX satellite. We navigated through the maze of illusions in the carnival mission like a team. We bonded. Remember?"

Desmond yawned.

"You *really* don't remember me? I thought we made a good team. The Agency thought so too. That's why they made us partners."

"We're not partners!" Desmond quickly interrupted the babbling tech whiz.

"Sure, we are."

"I work alone."

"It's not what the Agency wants. It's me and you from here on out, Super. The dynamic duo. We can start fresh. From the very beginning. Get to know each other."

Desmond was clearly becoming annoyed.

"Want to know what my hobbies are?"

"What I want to know is where Billy Bob Billy Jeff Jenkins is hiding."

The computer geek nodded. "OK. Fair enough. We can bond later. Plenty of time for that." Sabio turned off his eight-track player and pounded on the dashboard. The console came undone, extending outward and then flipping over to reveal a computer monitor. A world map appeared on the screen. The flashy gadgetry seemed to take Desmond by surprise.

"Our friends at GEO COMM have no idea where he is. But we suspect he's somewhere in the desert."

"I guess that makes sense." Desmond studied the screen. "Where else can you have a successful launch?"

"Correct, but which desert? And where do we start looking?" Sabio tapped the screen. Every known desert filled the monitor, along with snapshots of terrain information. Some had deep valleys and rivers, while others had caves.

"With only four days, who knows what we'll find—if we find anything at all. We're completely in the dark." Sabio turned the steering wheel left, biting down on his lip, until the road straightened out.

"We're not completely in the dark."

"What do you mean?"

"The footage."

"What about it?"

"Think back to it," Desmond said, looking at Sabio, acknowledging his plus-size presence for the first time since setting foot inside the van. The two shared a glance, and as if by some unseen connection, Sabio was able to read Desmond's mind.

"OCTO!" Sabio shouted. "I knew it! I knew it! I knew it!" He pounded the dashboard. The cargo van swerved. Desmond took hold of the steering wheel, trying to center the van back into its lane.

"Those were OCTO soldiers in the video. Not unknown militia. Only they could've pulled something like that," Sabio continued, and took back control of the steering wheel once the excitement wore down. The cargo van drove straight again.

"But if OCTO is involved, then that means—"

"The Black Hand is involved," Desmond added.

"And if the Black Hand is involved, then that means—"

"War." The words were said without hesitation.

"War." Sabio uttered the same words under his breath.

The two grew quiet when it dawned on them that the mission was the makings of something grander, far darker than they had predicted.

The Black Hand was a powerful entity with unlimited reach. There was no part of the world it could not touch, no political party it could not influence, no world leader it could not assassinate, no man or woman it could not buy. For this reason, many came from out of the shadows to bow and pledge unbent fealty to the dark one, adding mischief to the world and to the ever-growing surplus of militias, weapons, hidden bases, and financial support. Everyone in the Agency knew the Black Hand stood at the apex of its era, poised to conquer the world. Yet, for whatever reason, it did nothing. It allowed its minions to run havoc across continents, scarcely making any gains. It spent millions on world-domination schemes, only to be thwarted by the Agency. It allowed many of its bases to be captured and its technology used for the purpose of good. The Agency speculated that the Black Hand was simply having fun with the world and biding its time for the right moment to strike. But world leaders argued that the Black Hand was not real. A made-up story created by a young-radical organization, in the hopes of instilling fear and chaos. Whatever the reasons were, the Agency had always known that there would be a day when the Black Hand would make its first move. That day was yesterday, with OCTO, the Black Hand's private militia. They were fierce, brutal, and savagely trained to kill without remorse. They were rarely seen, and those who came in contact with them had the misfortune of succumbing to a painful and brutal death. Billy Bob Billy Jeff Jenkins's exfiltration by the elite squad meant that he had been chosen as part of a master plan that involved total world annihilation. He'd made this abundantly clear with his crude PowerPoint presentation depicting missile strikes.

"Do you believe the Black Hand is real?" Sabio asked curiously, his worried tone breaking the silence.

It was a question that everyone in the Agency was too afraid to answer although knowing what the answer was.

In that moment, Sabio noted the expression on Desmond's face. It was serious, and still, eyes wide open as if something unspeakable peeked inside his mind.

"Yes," Desmond responded.

"So, it's finally making its move after all these years? What I've never understood is why it hates us so much. People, I mean. Why all the rage? And why use people to help? Isn't it contradicting itself?"

Desmond said nothing.

"And why now? Why make a move all of a sudden? Why not last week or last year?"

"Don't know. But I bet Billy Bob does."

"Good point. You hungry?"

The cargo van pulled alongside the desert highway into a remote ma-and-pa shop. The store was outfitted with a cracked wood exterior, a screen door, dust-stained windows, and a carved-wood sign that hung crookedly above the front door with the misshapen words *Ma and Pa Grocery*. The small structure was no different from all the others they had seen littered across the desert highway, deteriorating under the scorching sun, only this one had a slanted porch and was serving food.

Sabio came out of the store, biting down on a sandwich. He joined the Superspy, who stood alongside the van, gazing out into the desert. He handed Desmond a second sandwich, wrapped in wax paper. It was bigger than his hand and thicker than his clenching fist.

"It's good. Eat it," Sabio assured him with a mouth full of ham and cheese.

Desmond took a peek inside and found turkey, ham, cheese, lettuce, tomatoes, alfalfa, and all kinds of gooey dressing. He took a bite and immediately agreed with Sabio. The flavors were overwhelming. They chewed quietly while admiring the desert scenery. The distant rocky hills showed the desert's age through soft, grainy, orange-brown-and-white striations. In some places, the striations crumbled on top of each other, meshing beautifully into a swirl of colors.

"Makes you wonder what will happen to all of this if those rockets hit, don't it?"

Desmond stopped chewing. For a brief moment the landscape had made him forget who he was and why he was out here. Sabio's words had brought him back. Desmond tucked away the desire to be normal and became the Superspy again. "Any hunches?" he asked.

"No. Well, actually, yes, but no." Sabio noticed the confused expression on Desmond's face. "Yes," he finally admitted and took a bite of his sandwich. "It's kind of complicated."

"Try me."

The tech genius opened the back door to his cargo van, leaving Desmond to behold the sight of gadgetry, monitors, and computer mainframes that a hardware junkie needed to be called a tech genius.

"Close the door."

Desmond walked inside and closed the door behind him. Sabio sat down and cracked his knuckles, and with the flick of a switch, the two men found themselves bathed in dazzling lights and high-powered air conditioning.

Sabio held the remaining sandwich in his mouth while he typed away erratically. He pulled up records of many known associates affiliated with the redneck scientist. Desmond was impressed. It seemed that Sabio was actually good for something other than constant babbling.

"I created a database of people who have been involved with Mr. Billy Bob redneck extraordinaire. And each time, one name keeps popping up."

Sabio hit return, filling every screen with a blurry image of a male figure, dressed in what appeared to be hunting gear.

Desmond smirked. "Could've told you that without all this fancy tech stuff."

"But you didn't. The fancy tech stuff told me instead. I was surprised when I found out who he really was."

"It doesn't do us any good. He's dead."

"Is he really?" Sabio turned to Desmond, and the two minds became connected again.

"He's not?"

"Nope. Not dead—hiding." Sabio refocused his attention to his computer and typed a different command. A mountain region popped up. "Compounds. Gunfire. Feuds. Total isolation."

"No different than any other end-of-the-world sanctuary full of gun nuts."

"True, but this one's different. There are reports of an antisocial, highly skilled marksman living in a compound deep in the woods. He's been spotted leaving his hidden sanctuary only to pick up an order of"—Sabio paused for effect—"authentic Mexican food."

"How authentic?"

"Squirrel enchilada."

"That's not authentic Mexican food."

"He thinks it is."

Again, Desmond was impressed. Sabio was earning bonus points.

"Not bad for your new partner, huh?"

But he still found him annoying.

"If the Black Hand is really behind this, and if Billy Bob Billy Jeff Jenkins is part of its master plan, then he"—Sabio pointed to the fuzzy image of the male—"without a doubt is on their list and should be the first on ours."

Desmond leaned over to the screen and studied the map of the region. His eyes then shifted to the fuzzy image of the male figure in hunting gear. If there was anyone in the world besides the Black Hand who knew the whereabouts of Billy Bob Billy Jeff Jenkins, it would have to be the defunct man known as TJBJ—a man whose one passion in life had always been authentic Mexican food. But in a sad twist of fate has never actually experienced authentic Mexican food. He was known to confuse advertised Mexican junk food as the real thing, and the real thing, according to him, was always *muy sabroso*. If you tried to tell him otherwise, your body was quickly pumped with hot lead.

Chapter 5

Calling Mr. Dorkhovich

Had it been left up to Jeanine, the veteran nurse would have written off Mr. Dorkhovich the minute she saw him wheelchaired through the front doors of the Sunny Side Retirement Center some thirty-odd years ago. Now, some thirty-odd years later, she was convinced more than ever that the man was absolutely and positively dead.

Mr. Dorkhovich was a frail man at ninety-two, made up entirely of skin and bones with dark blemishes throughout his body, mostly centered around his eyes and face. He was bald, with a few thin grays freckled across the surface of his egg-shaped head and horizontal grooves cut deeply into his forehead to make the argument that, at one point in time, Mr. Dorkhovich was a methodical man of pure decision making. Time, however, had proven to be unkind to the methodical-thinking man. It robbed him of mobility and left him a bedridden relic with a mouth always ajar, accompanied by slow, rasping breaths, without the energy to speak—if speech was ever a part of his palate. The man had yet to grunt or utter a word in his thirty-odd years of existence at Sunny Side.

Not that Jeanine should have been surprised. The fifty-two-year-old veteran nurse had seen much in her years at Sunny Side, and Mr. Dorkhovich was nothing special. She was, however, struck at the unusual peculiarity possessed by the Russian's eyes. They were a faded blue, lacking the high contrast and vibrancy that came from the window to one's soul. *They* were expressionless. *He* was expressionless. Never a blink of discomfort or appreciation. Never a hint of like or dislike. When he was spoon-fed, he chewed and swallowed mechanically, devoid of any sentiment. When he was wheelchaired through the retirement grounds known for their beautiful olive trees and rose gardens, Mr. Dorkhovich never cracked a smile. *He* was lifeless. His *eyes* were lifeless, and each and every time Jeanine peered into their empty, blue, faded gaze, she was convinced, more than anything, just like on the very first day, that Mr.

Dorkhovich wasn't even there. The man was clearly dead; only his body failed to make the connection and continued pumping oxygen and blood through the frail, empty shell.

At the end of every month, a woman in her late sixties who could best be described as foreign and anomalous would be found sitting alongside Mr. Dorkhovich's bed. *Found* was the key word here because nobody, not even Jeanine, could attest to her monthly arrival at the nursing home. She was simply there with a visitor's badge that no one from Reception remembered issuing. She wasn't family because Mr. Dorkhovich had no family. She was, as his trust fund described, his personal assistant, who went only by Elena. The personal assistant stood five-feet-tall, with shoulder-length black hair and thick glasses, and sported the same recognizable long gray skirt and dark blouse from her previous visits. She acknowledged the nursing staff with her usual nod and thick Russian-accented *hellos*. She carried the same serious expression wherever she walked and never lent herself out for small talk, keeping the conversation curt with a simple nod, yes or no.

In short, Elena was cold company. She was courteous in her own cold way, keeping mostly to her cold self with her visits lasting an hour and only an hour, right down to the millisecond. Her clockwork visits convinced Jeanine that Elena was here on business, and business had been conducted in the form of reading for the past thirty-some years.

That's all Elena did. She'd sit and read to Mr. Dorkhovich from the leather-bound manuscript she grasped religiously. You would never find the one without the other. The two were inseparable. Elena clutched the manuscript tightly against her breast and protected it as a mother would a child. And when she read from its pages, a poet would emerge. Her signature pale expression was immediately replaced by a face flushed with color that conveyed the passion in her words. The sound of her voice played out beautifully, like a melody that tickled the auditory senses of everyone far and near, never failing to create a smile each and every time.

This was the only time that Jeanine and the nursing staff were convinced that Elena was not a robot but actually human, with warm blood coursing through her hard-to-see veins. Whenever Elena read, the nursing staff would gather quietly outside the room to listen. No one understood Russian, and no one really cared. It all sounded so wonderful. The staff would listen endlessly until Jeanine would spot them from around the corner and boot them back to work. Unlike the rest, the veteran nurse wasn't impressed by the scene. She grew angry at it each time. The passion conveyed through Elena's words was undoubtedly beautiful, but the words were falling onto dead ears. Mr. Dorkhovich never flinched. Not once. If it wasn't obvious before, then it should have been obvious now that this man was dead. No one could resist showing some spark of emotion at such spoken words.

"You're wasting your time," Jeanine blurted out one day while Elena read from her manuscript.

Elena paused midsentence and looked up at the rectangular-shaped blond nurse reclining so casually against the doorway.

"He can't hear you. He isn't there."

"I can assure you," Elena said in her cold, colorless, thick Russian accent, "Mr. Dorkhovich hears everything." She returned to her book.

Just like that, as mysterious as her arrival was, her departure was just the same. Elena vanished into thin air, manuscript and all. Not to be seen again till the following month.

The phone call came in the middle of the month on a gray, cloudy Sunday afternoon. It happened at lunchtime, as Jeanine was busy feeding her other patient, Mrs. Rosalie, who was seventy-years-old and could never sit still long enough to be spoon-fed.

"Please, Mrs. Rosalie," Jeanine begged. "Don't you want your pea soup?"

"No!" Mrs. Rosalie clamped her mouth shut and squirmed in her chair like an infant.

"You have to eat something. Food makes you strong. Don't you want to be strong?"

"No." Mrs. Rosalie swiped the spoon away from Jeanine's hand, rattling loudly the instant it hit the floor.

"Jeanine!"

Jeanine looked up, a hint of frustration still on her face. She saw Susan walking briskly from the middle of the hallway, stopping short of the cafeteria door to catch her breath.

"Been looking all over for you," Susan gasped.

"What is it?" Jeanine picked the spoon off the floor.

"Phone call."

"Take a message. I'm busy at the moment."

"It's for Mr. Dorkhovich."

The news took Jeanine by surprise. In the thirty-plus-odd years that she had taken care of the empty-gazed, saliva-dripping, lifeless man, no one had ever called for him. Not even Elena. Jeanine looked around the room, finding Sara only a few feet away.

"Sara, you mind?" she asked.

"No. Go ahead. I got this." Sara took over feeding Mrs. Rosalie while Jeanine and Susan walked back to Reception to discover what the phone call was about.

"Hello, this is Jeanine," she said calmly.

"Mr. Dorkhovich, please." The voice was also calm—and Russian.

"Who may I ask is calling?"

"A friend," the voice proclaimed.

"One minute, please." She placed the call on hold.

"Who is it?"

"A friend."

"Mr. Dorkhovich doesn't have any friends," Susan reminded the veteran nurse.

"Apparently, he has one." Jeanine shrugged and casually made her way down the hallway.

She stopped short of Mr. Dorkhovich's room and peered inside. As usual, there lay the lifeless bed lump, fixated on the ceiling, his chest slowly sinking and rising, trailed by rasping, gurgling breaths.

"Mr. Dorkhovich." Jeanine stepped foot inside the room. "You have a phone call. Would you like to take the call?" She snickered— more like laughed.

As if a light switch had been flipped from out of nowhere, Mr. Dorkhovich blinked for the first time in thirty-odd years. His eyes became unglued from the ceiling and rotated slowly toward Jeanine. With the slight turn from his neck came the sound of crackling bone. Saliva dripped from the corners of his mouth as his lips stretched backward into what appeared to be a smirk.

A cold shiver raced through Jeanine's body. The hairs from the back of her neck stood up as the person she'd presumed dead for over thirty years met her gaze halfway through the room with a feverish smirk.

How many times had she mocked him that he was dead? How many times had she snapped her fingers close to his face to force a reaction? How many times had she told him he was a waste of bed space? A waste of time? And how many times had she poked fun at his frail body?

The questions went on and on inside her head while she helped the frail man into his wheelchair.

Mr. Dorkhovich hears everything.

She heard Elena's voice. In that moment, Jeanine looked at Mr. Dorkhovich and was greeted by a pair of wild, blue, faded eyes and that same overzealous smirk that refused to leave his face.

Jeanine wheeled Mr. Dorkhovich down the hallway toward Reception. She parked him alongside the counter and pressed the phone up against his ear, with Susan watching quietly. Mr. Dorkhovich reached up with trembling fingers and snatched the phone away from his nurse.

"*Dobryj Dyen'*," he said in a low, raspy voice. Susan and Jeanine shared the same look of shock and surprise after hearing the man speak for the very first time.

The voice on the other end spoke. Mr. Dorkhovich listened intently. His eyes shifted from left to right. His face became twisted and contorted into what appeared to be a smile. Saliva drooled all over the floor when his head rocked back uncontrollably from a burst of laughter that could be heard down the hallway, rebounding into every open bedroom to make the announcement that Mr. Dorkhovich was alive. He was still chuckling when Jeanine wheelchaired him back into his room. He was still chuckling after she tucked him gingerly into his bed and placed the covers over him. His wild eyes were looking no longer at her but through her, at a deep dark secret that had been revealed to him and only him.

Mr. Dorkhovich vanished the very next day, leaving Sunny Side in full-on panic mode. The staff searched rooms, bathrooms, closets, laundry chutes, basements, trash cans, dumpsters, and anything they could think of that a crazy ninety-two-year-old man who had just come back to life could crawl himself into. The police found nothing useful when they searched his room. And they were met with utter silence by the nursing staff when they inquired about the old patron. It turned out that no one knew anything about the man. With no leads to go by other than a mysterious phone call and a woman who appeared and disappeared into thin air at the end of every month, the police left Sunny Side with no particular findings.

At roughly the same time, Jeanine walked the empty hallways with a dreadful task in mind. The thought of searching Mr. Dorkhovich's room was a displeasing one, but who best to look for clues than the person who had taken care of him for thirty-some-odd years? Let's not also forget, the person who had mocked him repeatedly for those same years. With her luck, she'd find him waiting at his bedside, standing upright, with a sharp knife in hand and that devilish grin plastered all over his face.

Mr. Dorkhovich hears everything.

"Come on…get a grip," she uttered under her own breath.

She cared nothing for the man but cared deeply for the nursing staff. She didn't want to see anyone get blamed or fired for his unusual departure. When she arrived at his room, she hesitated by the door and took a deep breath. When she was ready, she tiptoed her way inside and stopped the minute she reached the center of the small space. She took a careful look around. The room was plain white, lacking any character, pictures, books, or clues as to who Mr. Dorkhovich was. The closet and bathroom doors had been left open from the day's investigation, and his dresser had only one gown inside. The part of the man that still lingered inside came from the outline left on his bed. Nothing more. Jeanine had seen enough. There was nothing useful in the room. She turned back around slowly, praying he wasn't standing by the door like in the horror movies, wielding a knife. When the coast was clear, she walked out as quietly as she'd walked in.

After ten days, Mr. Dorkhovich had been declared missing and presumed dead. With no one coming forward to make a big stink about the missing ninety-two-year-old man, the nursing staff at Sunny Side received no backlash from the authorities. No one had made a big stink about Elena either. For the very first time in over thirty-odd years, Elena had failed to show up at the end of the month. Much like Mr. Dorkhovich, the personal assistant had vanished mysteriously without a trace.

A month after his disappearance, as Jeanine wheelchaired Mrs. Rosalie back to her room from the gardens, she found the door to Mr. Dorkhovich's room wide open. There had been stories circulating about Elena among the nursing staff: her ghost had been seen inside the room, reading to Mr. Dorkhovich's bed. These were, of course, stories. No one really knew what had happened to the Russian pair, and to say that Elena was also dead was an exaggeration. Still, the nursing staff found the story humorous, and although the room had been labeled off limits, they'd occasionally manage a quick peek inside during their breaks and lunch in the hopes of stumbling on to something. Jeanine was no different. The veteran nurse had been caught stealing a quick glance or two during her rounds. But she had never found the door left wide open before. There was also something unusual about the room. Come to think of it, she had spotted it rather easily, as though it had been set up just for her. Jeanine plucked it from the pillow. Her eyes couldn't believe what she was holding. She had been mesmerized by it for years and never let on to anyone that it piqued her interest. Only Elena knew, after she caught Jeanine glancing at it from time to time. Jeanine searched the room for answers. There were none. She searched the hallways with her newly discovered treasure tucked safely inside her scrubs, leaving poor old Mrs. Rosalie alone in her wheelchair. Still no answers. Just an empty hallway.

Was this a prank? Or had Elena truly been here?

The answer would take her four hours north into the mountains, and into *Beskeden*. The tucked-away village was just as Jeanine had remembered it: small, colorful, bustling with storefronts advertising a wide variety of knickknacks that provided an insight into the Danish past. That's what Beskeden was: a snapshot into the past with cobblestone roads, carriages, wood houses, gas lanterns, and townsfolk who dressed from a time of simple ideology that echoed the humble beginnings of small towns everywhere before modernization.

The town stood within the confines of green fields and unobstructed blue skies, boasting the agrarian lifestyle. The windmill at the center of town symbolized the humility that Beskeden stood for. But it also symbolized the true reason why so many tourists endured the four-hour pilgrimage to the boring Danish past. Directly below its sails lay its wine and pastry shops. Every store featured a different take on exotic wine. Every pastry tasted a little different from its neighbor. There was nothing like it anywhere, and for that reason many came from all parts of the country to get a little tipsy from the myriad of exotic wines and cakes that Beskeden was known for.

The delicacies would have to wait this time. Jeanine had not come for them. She had come for the bookstore. The only bookstore in the Danish village, or anywhere else that she knew of, that housed Russian literature. How a Russian bookstore had ended up in a small Danish village was a mystery to her, and one that the townsfolk did not speak openly about. In fact, the townsfolk didn't care for it much, given the fact that the bookstore did not lend itself to Danish tradition or sell anything Danish. The town of Beskeden had decided to distance itself from it by pretending it didn't exist.

Jeanine needed the townsfolk to remember. She had stumbled upon it drunk in her last visit and wasn't having much luck finding it this time around. Her inquiries required a little persuasion in the form of cash. After several wine tastings, pastry samplings, and coerced Danish knickknack purchases, the townsfolk miraculously remembered the Russian bookstore. She was pointed two streets down from the plaza to an alleyway full of stacked crates and garbage cans.

The storefront was a single black steel door with nothing to indicate that it was a bookstore. The door had to be painstakingly pulled apart from its rusted metal frame to reveal a dark, narrow maze of stacked book columns. The maze led Jeanine to the back of the store, where the old shopkeeper sat behind his desk. He smiled at the nurse as though he were welcoming an old friend he had not seen in years. He greeted her in Russian.

"Hi, there." Jeanine returned the smile. "Can you translate a book for me?"

It was obvious the old shopkeeper didn't understand a word of English. He continued smiling with a hint of confusion.

"Book," Jeanine said slowly and pointed to the stack of books behind her. "Can you translate a Russian book for me?"

The old shopkeeper continued to smile and said nothing.

"Book...book." She reached into her purse and pulled out Elena's leather manuscript. "Can you translate this book for me into English? I don't read Russian." She handed it to the shopkeeper, who glanced at the faded leather cover with curious eyes.

He leafed through the pages carefully and said nothing. This was not the reaction Jeanine had been expecting. She was waiting for him to break into song and dance, the way Elena had for so many years. No, the old shopkeeper became furious at the turn of every page. Before reaching the end, he slammed the book shut and handed it back to Jeanine. He gestured at her to leave.

"What? Why?"

The old man yelled at her.

"I don't understand what you're saying."

When she didn't move, the shopkeeper jumped up from behind his desk and dragged her away by the elbow, knocking over book columns.

"You're hurting me!" she protested.

Jeanine was pushed hard into the alley. Before the shopkeeper had a chance to shut the metal door, she wedged her foot inside, keeping a narrow slit open between the two. This angered the old man, who protested at her belligerently.

"I'm not leaving until you tell me what this says." She held up the book as close to his face as the door would allow.

The shopkeeper released a sigh of frustration. He pursed his lips together; from the look on his face, there was something he wanted desperately to say but found the words difficult to pronounce.

"The...Black...Hand...rises," the shopkeeper squeezed out in broken English. He then kicked Jeanine's foot from under the door and locked it shut.

The Black Hand? What is the Black Hand? The words stumped her all the way back home.

The nursing staff at Sunny Side were shocked when they heard the gruesome details surrounding Jeanine's death. Her body had been discovered against the corner of her bedroom after she had gone missing for a week. It had been pounded ferociously into a bloody heap of raw meat and bones, leaving no shape of the person it once had been. In the nurse's own blood, the shape of a bloodied hand had been drawn above her body, with the words *he hears everything* scribbled in Russian.

The homicide baffled the police—as did the enormous hole along the side of the house and the giant, bloodied footprint the size of a midsize car leading into the street. Elena's manuscript, unbeknown to police, was nowhere to be found.

Chapter 6

Freeland

If you were in search of a place that put you in absolute control of your destiny by doing away with the influences of the Western world, including that widely popular notion of globalization, then Freeland was the place for you. It wasn't on any map, but it was undoubtedly out there like a rare coarse diamond, unpolished by the spinning gears of modernization. Admission to the reclusive and exclusive land came in only two options: the first, option A, involved a six-figure down payment in exchange for clues to where Freeland may or may not be, whereas option B relied heavily on sheer wit and plain old-fashioned luck as you were tasked with finding the location yourself. If you chose option B, as was the case with most considering how broke and desperate many had to be to want to start their lives anew, the scavenger hunt led you east into a scorching sun, desert roads, wilderness trails, abandoned logging ruts, and scattered corpses of would-be Freeland seekers before stumbling across an uncharted highway that took you farther east into the promised land—home to the off-the-grid folk.

Off-the-grid folk was a term used to describe Freelanders. It stood right alongside *free folk* and *liberator* but not so far away from *paranoid* and *delusional*. Freelanders had chosen seclusion as a way of life by living off the land, convinced that at some point in time, the powers that be would bring an end to the world. And when that time finally came, they would be ready to take possession of the earth, for they had already begun to live a life free of Western capitalist influence, surrounding themselves instead with the one thing in life that mattered most, the *only* thing that could secure absolute control over one's own destiny and provide a means to all things absolute: *guns*. Big-heavy-shiny-loud guns that caused big-ugly-fiery deaths and explosions with occasional dismemberments.

All Freelanders treasured their big-heavy-shiny-loud guns. They were needed to protect their second-most valuable possession: privacy. Freelanders weren't too keen with outsiders. They wanted to be left alone, and anyone who trespassed upon their sacred land with the intent of asking questions was shot first and questioned later if he or she were still breathing. Needless to say, the Freeland community were of criminal background and made up entirely of the redneck class because of the adjacent redneck states.

Sabio's intel had only vague imagery of TJBJ's compound in a wilderness setting. What Desmond needed was a starting point with a finger pointing in the next direction. With its reputation and backwoods scenery, Freeland had become that starting point, and one that Desmond felt strongly about. A part of that certainty was also owed to George's diner. It was the only highway eatery close to Freeland that advertised a flavorful palate of authentic Mexican food via makeshift road signs scattered across the highway. It was impossible not to salivate over the mental images of hot, steamy, gooey Mexican food served on a hot plate after a long road trek to nowhere. The temptation to pull over loomed heavy and large on anyone wanting to bite down on soft, chewy, slow-cooked, spicy meat, only to have it explode inside your mouth with flavors so rich it would have you speaking Spanish fluently until the savory taste went away. But in truth, George's wasn't actually serving authentic Mexican food. Whatever it was serving had the word Mexican attached to the front of every food menu item ending mostly in possum, deep-fried possum, deep-fried roadkill, deep-fried roadkill surprise, squirrel enchilada, and donkey grilled burritos.

Stumbling upon George's confirmed to Desmond and Sabio that they were on the right path. Seclusion and misinterpreted Mexican food always equaled TJBJ. He was, of course, a redneck but of a special breed.

With the van entering Freeland, the dynamic duo were greeted with rolling hills plastered against a cobalt-blue sky. The lush green fields of knee-high grass spread out for miles and miles without so much as an artificial structure to obscure the natural setting of land meeting sky. But after so many miles, the land had still to produce any signs of life, and yet there was that unsettling feeling that you were being watched from way atop the hills. The cargo van made for a silvery eyesore against a pool of emerald green that traversed horizontally across the highway, much like a duck in a carnival shooting gallery. It was as an advertised target for easy pickings to anyone looking to end a dry spell of gunfire. When gunfire failed to show itself after a few miles, the road bottlenecked close into the hills, so close that Desmond could reach out from the window to feel the fragile grass rush past his fingertips. The duo were convinced that at any moment, the van would be ambushed by trigger-happy folk. They held their breaths and watched their surroundings closely, Sabio with trembling hands, Desmond anxious and ready with his pistol by his side. As the road opened back up to blue sky and gave itself away to open wilderness, they both drew a sigh of relief. Sabio checked his pants for wet stains. To his relief, there were none.

The road took them into the thick wilderness where trees loomed heavy and large, and the road became uneven from the lack of smooth surfaces. The van rocked from side to side and curved downward, tossing the men inside as a dryer would a load of laundry. When the van reached the flat bottom, the maze of the wilderness came into full view with multiple paths leading everywhere. Maybe they'd go right. Maybe they'd go left. Maybe they'd go up the path. Maybe they'd go down the path. A sharp turn here, a sharp turn there, and on and on like a secret combination that would unlock the mystery of the forest, with TJBJ as the end reward.

Much to the duo's surprise, the road did not end with TJBJ. It brought them to something unexpected that forced Sabio to stop the car and turn to Desmond with the same look of bewilderment that was plastered all over his face.

"Slow," Desmond commanded, not taking his eyes off the windshield.

Sabio nodded and put the van back in gear, treading slowly, remaining cautious of his newfound discovery. Desmond pulled out his pistol and kept it close to his chest.

The wilderness maze of wonders had brought the team into a ghost town, centered around a medium-size clearing. The town was two miles long and four buildings wide. A paved road ran through the middle of town, flanked by dilapidated shops lining both sides of the street.

"This doesn't make any sense," Sabio said quietly while examining the buildings. "For people wanting nothing to do with the outside world, they sure have a funny way of showing it."

Sabio was right. The shops were out of place. The paved road was a luxury. The nonworking streetlights and loose-hanging powerlines spoke of capitalism and synergy in the form of a modest economy that had at one point appeared to be vibrant and living.

"It's always the case that people come together to establish some norm. Even if that norm is something they once knew and despised," Desmond responded. Sabio agreed with a single grunt.

Desmond could imagine off-the-grid folk coming together from the hilltops to create what they considered to be a perfect society. He could imagine everyone sitting down to draft a constitution to live and die by, with a modest economy to feed off. He could imagine the townsfolk living among each other, happily at first, till the fighting would start because someone thought or spoke differently. Then the fighting would lead to killing by big-heavy-shiny-loud guns till everyone went their separate ways and abandoned it all. It was a theory that turned factual when the duo took notice of the bullet holes, burnt rooftops, shattered windows, and scorched cars that littered the small town. Freeland stood as the starting and ending point of it all. A feeble attempt at coexistence, now quiet and abandoned. Or so he thought.

Forty feet away, nestled against the base of a hill and separate from the ghost town, lay the only undamaged building with working lights. It was a tavern, made obvious by the sign directly above the front door that said *Tavern*. Faded white exterior, chipped paint, with a skewed wood structure that advertised a building collapse in a not-so-distant future, the tavern stood as the only remaining relic of the fallout and a return to Western ideals publicized by the piece of torn cardboard nailed next to the front door with the words *cash only* scribbled across it. Someone desperately wanted to get out of this town.

"Would cash actually exist in a place like this?" Sabio asked, staring at the sign.

"No. That's why you trade." Desmond was referencing the second sign, right below the first, which advertised traded goods.

Sabio parked the van and took his seat belt off. Desmond got out and shook his head at his partner, who sank back down on his seat and locked the door. The Superspy took in the town in one sweeping view. The feeling that they were being watched was stronger this time around. There was probably a gun pointed at his head. Or worse, his genitals. Desmond turned his attention back to the tavern and walked inside.

The front door announced Desmond's arrival with a loud, elongated squeak. The five patrons at the bar, decked out in hunting gear, paused from their drinking and turned around to look at what had wandered inside. Desmond remained still, unsure of what was about to happen. He could see questions forming all over their curious faces. After a dragged-out moment, one of the patrons burped. The men went back to their drinking.

Desmond took this as *hello* and *welcome to nowhere*.

The Superspy walked across the room to a corner booth, the weight of his hiking boots causing the floorboards to creak loudly. He sat down, not noticing the layers of dust that had settled on his clothes. He swatted the cushions and blew on the table top, causing the dust to poof into a cloud of dancing particles that were instantly drawn to his face. Desmond coughed and waved the dust away as he took in the tavern much like he had the town. It was small, covered in shadow by ceiling lights that couldn't decide whether to stay on or off. From the looks of it all, the tavern had served as someone's home once before it was torn inside out and outfitted with a broad circular bar and six table booths that lined the opposite ends of the room.

The waitress came lazily toward Desmond, chewing her gum loudly. She had wavy brown hair, torn jeans, flip-flops, and a sleeveless sweat shirt with the word *boss* written across it in faded red. She looked midforties, blowing out smoke from her cigarette, annoyed by the sight of the outsider.

"Help you?" she said in a voice raspy from a lifetime of smoking, and raised both eyebrows.

"Water?"

"Unless water means beer, we ain't got no water here. Only beer."

The men at the bar chuckled.

"I'll have a beer, then."

She nodded in disgust. When she returned, she tossed down a stained-glass-mug with mysterious floating chunks.

"Fifty dollars," she demanded.

"That's pretty expensive beer."

"Only beer in town, *honey*. I brew it myself," she snorted, and then snatched the money from Desmond's hand. She turned and was about to leave.

"I'm looking for someone."

"No kidding. I'm looking for someone too." She planted both hands on the table and leaned into Desmond's face. "I'm looking for you to hurry the hell up with that drink and get the hell out of here."

The men laughed again.

"He lives somewhere around here."

"Look around you, *sweet cheeks*. Does it look like anyone lives around here? No one lives around here. You're in the middle of nowhere. Ain't that right, fellas?"

The men at the bar raised their glasses and cheered.

"The person that I'm looking for likes to carry a gun."

She blew out smoke and then magically pulled a gun out of thin air. "You mean like this one?"

"A very big gun."

She reached around her waist and pulled out a Magnum revolver. "Like this one? Is this it? This the one you looking for? We all carry guns around here, *cinnamon tush*. And we don't like it"—suddenly her hand swayed the barrel of the gun at Desmond's head—"when people not from around these parts begin to ask a lot of stupid questions."

Desmond noticed the men had stopped drinking and were now looking in his direction. Everything had gone silent.

"Anything else you wish to ask, my *dark-chocolate friend*?" She blew smoke in his face.

"No."

"Good. Then hurry up and get the hell out of my bar."

The waitress walked away. The men went back to drinking.

"Actually, there is one more thing."

The waitress stopped, turned around, and cocked her gun.

"The guy I'm looking for. He loves Mexican food."

The waitress's face went cold. Her gum chewing stopped. Everyone at the bar spat out their beers. Dead silence filled the tiny room again.

"Ain't no Mexican food around here," she responded, without the sass this time, a little nervous.

"Oh, I know that. And you know that. But you see…he doesn't know that. In fact"—Desmond picked up his drink, sniffed it, and set it back down in disgust—"he wouldn't be able to tell the difference between what is and what isn't. And there's a place not far from here that sells a mutated form of what isn't Mexican food. I have no doubt he's been there plenty of times and been down here a few times, sitting at your bar, enjoying his food, waiting on you to serve him his drink from that stool over there that no one seems to mind." Everyone turned to the stool that was a gem in comparison to the others: sparkling clean, waited on by two pristine mugs and a tray full of peppermint candy. A placard rested on top of the seat with the word *RESERVED* scribbled across its shiny metal facade.

"I think you better leave," she said nervously.

"And I think you need to tell me where he is."

"I don't know what you're talking about."

Desmond laid out a wad of cash on the table: $5,000, to be exact. He lined up every bill nice and neat so that everyone could see.

The waitress's eyes lit up. She took a few forward steps to take it all in.

"That is more than enough money for anyone looking to get out of here. I just need to know where my friend is."

The waitress said nothing, still hypnotized by the green, crisp cash.

"He goes by TJBJ," Desmond finally added.

A bar patron stood up, his stool scraping hard against the floorboards. He looked at Desmond, then at the waitress, and left. Another stood up and left right after. And then another.

"There ain't..." The waitress slowly backed away from the money, her eyes longing for it. "There ain't no one here by that name, mister. You should leave. And don't look back," she said in a low voice. She was frightened. Her hands were trembling. Her cigarette had fallen out of her mouth and onto the floor without her even noticing.

The remaining bar patrons stood up to leave. Desmond watched as they exited the door one by one. Once they were gone, he focused his attention back to the waitress, who had disappeared. The back door was wide open.

Desmond scooped up the cash and rushed out the back door into a zigzagging maze of narrow buildings, fences, and short alleyways. She wasn't far. He could hear running steps a short distance away. Desmond cranked up the speed and turned the corner, letting his adrenaline get the better of him, scaling over fences, turning unchecked corners until—

Click!

He came to a complete stop.

"That's far enough," a dark shape whispered, aiming what appeared to be a gun. Desmond raised both hands into the air.

"Give it here. All of it." The shape motioned nervously with its gun.

Desmond lowered his hands and reached inside his jacket.

"Slow," the shape demanded, taking careful aim at Desmond's head. Desmond pulled out the wad of cash and placed it carefully on the ground.

"Back up," the shape instructed.

Desmond did as he was told.

The dark shape took two careful forward steps, knelt down cautiously, and swept up the cash in one circular motion while keeping its gun aimed. It began counting the money immediately. "I hear you're looking for that lunatic. Why? You here to kill him?"

"Just need to talk to him."

"I was hoping you were here to kill him," the shape said, placing the money securely inside its breast pocket. "Turn around."

Desmond had no choice. He turned around.

"Now walk," it commanded. "Go back where you came from, and then keep right at the fork."

Desmond paused and listened carefully.

"You'll come across a tree. We call it crab tree—you'll see why when you find it. From there, it's up the ravine. Not much farther to Hidden Trails."

"Hidden Trails?"

"That's where you'll find that son of a bitch!"

Desmond could hear the aggression building up inside the shape's voice.

"It wasn't always like this," the shape continued. "It was all working just fine till he came. He ruined everything! Killed everyone. Killed my family. I got nothing left. No point in staying here anymore. I want justice, mister. We all do."

A noise came from somewhere in the distance. The dark shape quickly darted away and disappeared down the alley.

Desmond made his way back to the cargo van while keeping a vigilant eye on the surrounding buildings. Freeland had served its purpose. It was time to move on. Next stop was Hidden Trails.

The duo turned around and drove five miles back up the road, just like the shape had instructed. They kept right at the fork and caught sight of a disfigured tree that was in the shape of a crab. From there, Sabio made his way upstream, dead-ending into the base of a hill. There was no choice left but to hike.

Desmond strapped on his backpack and slung his assault rifle over his right shoulder. He tightened the knots on his boots and attached gas grenades to his utility belt. Sabio carefully wheeled out a drone the size of a small kitchen table from the back of his van. It was sleek, sexy, and made up entirely of black metal framing shaped to resemble a Harrier jet.

"Her name's Rosemarie." He pulled out his laptop and typed a set of commands. The drone roared to life, creating a strong whirlwind of dirt, leaves, and twigs over the two men. The computer whiz smiled at the sight of his own contraption.

"What are you doing?" Desmond screamed over the engines.

"Eyes on the sky," Sabio responded.

"I don't need that."

"But I do."

"But I don't! And I don't need you."

Rosemarie powered down. The men were showered by falling leaves, dirt, and twigs. Desmond could see the hurt expression on Sabio's face.

"What do you mean, you don't need me?"

"I work alone. I told you that."

"But we're a team."

Desmond shook his head.

"The Agency wants us working toge—"

"I don't care what the Agency wants. I know what I have to do to get it done, and I don't need you or...Rosemarie," Desmond gestured at the drone.

"But I've done good so far...haven't I?"

Desmond nodded.

"Then let me keep on doing what I'm doing."

"Too dangerous."

"I can do danger. I've been the lifelines in over two hundred missions. I've been able to remedy every situation and figure out any puzzle. I've been known to approach things calmly, methodically, rationally, systematically—"

"This isn't some phone call. This is as real as real gets. And I don't have time to be babysitting you. You'll just get in the way."

Sabio became quiet. The sort of quiet where one is hurting on the inside, about to cry.

"Look…just…stay in the van. I'll be back soon." Desmond turned and left. He began to make his way up the trail when he heard Sabio's distant voice.

"You know why I'm here? Why I'm really, really here?"

Desmond stopped, about to climb over a boulder. He turned around and sighed deeply; he didn't have time for this.

"Operation Hidden Vault."

The Superspy clenched his jaw and tightened his fists.

"The Agency felt it necessary to babysit the Superspy in case he decided to screw things up again. That's why I'm here. And this is my shot to prove to them that I'm more than just some guy on the phone. That I'm capable of becoming a real agent."

Desmond remained quiet, but after a minute he turned back around and made his way up the ravine. Sabio powered on Rosemarie and watched her hover above the trees.

As Desmond made his way into the woods he caught sight of the drone whoosh noisily across the sky. He groaned and wondered if anyone else had heard it too.

Chapter 7

Hidden Trails

Rosemarie flew high above the clouds into the azure sky. Its wings glistened brilliantly in the sun as it glided steadily against the wind, over miles and miles of uninhabited terrain that was Hidden Trails—another slice of redneck heaven, like Freeland, but with a slight difference. You were never alone at Hidden Trails. Its steep hills, venomous snakes, roaming bears, sporadic wildfires, and occasional landslides were your everyday companions. They never left your side and were willing and ready to introduce you to their constant companion, death. Meanwhile, forty miles up north in Freeland, you found yourself basking in the peace and tranquility of its natural setting, slurping on rabbit stew, with a plate of hog ribs and beans by your side without so much as a care in the world. It was no secret that off-the-grid folk preferred Freeland. The odds of staying alive were in your favor before a vengeful bullet from out of nowhere buried itself inside your skull. Still, it was a much-preferred outcome over the certain demise that awaited those at Hidden Trails.

Rosemarie swooped down and soared smoothly across the treetops, catching sight of Desmond's heat signature with its glass eye. He was a white shadow, encircled by gray tree shapes, studying something peculiar against a tree. Rosemarie zoomed in, catching a blurry glimpse of what appeared to be a sign as Desmond peeled it carefully away from the tree. He held it sensibly in his stands, studying it for what seemed a long time.

No trespassing or else.

The words were scribbled in black crayon across a torn piece of cardboard with a picture of a bullet-infested corpse pasted underneath.

This was all too familiar to Desmond. He had seen it before many years ago. Sweat trickled down his forehead. His fists tightened with anger. He was overwhelmed with mixed emotions until the distant whoosh from the unwelcome drone jetting across the sky snapped the Superspy out of his trance. He tossed the warning sign onto the ground and peered into the wilderness.

"I know you're here...somewhere," the Superspy whispered, studying the trees and hills for where that *somewhere* could possibly be.

Several bear sightings and poisonous snakes later, the unforgiveable terrain gave itself away to more pictures—only these were nailed not against a tree but against makeshift crosses rooted deeply into the ground, scattered in every direction. The victims in these photographs were the same as the first: mutilated by gunfire, strewn about the ground, their eyes wide in horror when they realized they were dying.

It wasn't always like this...it was all working fine till he came...he killed everyone.

Desmond heard the voice from the stranger in the alley echo inside his head. It made perfect sense that TJBJ showed up when Freeland was experiencing peace and prosperity. Then he began to open his big mouth, as was always the case, causing a fallout between the people till they came to their senses and realized who the true enemy really was. The end result was a last-ditch effort to rid themselves of TJBJ once and for all: a battle at Hidden Trails. But the Freelanders never stood a chance. They had no clue who they were up against. Even in great numbers and with all of them surviving the dangerous trek through the forest, they were doomed to fail. He killed them all, leaving their remains exactly where they fell. The pictures were his death cards, each with a mocking catchphrase: *dummy, stupid, never saw it coming, look out behind you, through the eye, splatter brains*. It was a tactic he liked to use to lure more victims into his crosshairs. Sadly, those victims were loved ones fueled by vengeance and empathy over their fallen kin.

The wave of mixed emotions from earlier struck harder this time. Desmond clamped his fists shut. He was experiencing shortness of breath. Sweat trickled down his forehead as his mind raced back to a few years ago. The Superspy was no stranger to TJBJ. He had captured the psychopathic killer years before, but only by sheer luck. He'd found him scarfing down a plate of Chihuahua nachos in a drabbed-out wannabe Mexican restaurant. They scuffled, equally matched when the nachos took a swing at TJBJ, giving him severe stomach pain and instant diarrhea. The redneck passed out and fell into the hands of the Agency.

How could a simple-minded fool from scrap beginnings emerge a champion marksman and become the deadliest sniper inside the Black Hand's repertoire? The Agency felt the answer lay in his diet. What exactly did the redneck elite sniper eat that made him so efficient at killing? Anal probes were ordered. Dozens and dozens of anal probes, and much to TJBJ's horrific girly screams of protest, they were inserted without remorse. When those turned up nothing, blood work was done that, surprisingly, yielded uncanny results. Before they could run further tests, the man had escaped via an unused drainage pipe and vowed vengeance. TJBJ created a hit list of those who did him wrong, and if your name was on it, then it was only a matter of time before you were torn to shreds by twelve-inch holes.

Thus, the manhunt had commenced: Operation Junk Food.

But the operation was failing. No one could locate the whereabouts of the missing elite sniper. As promised, names had begun to fall off his list with the daily discovery of bodies. Field agents were found at parks, malls, grocery stores, restaurants, in cars, in bed, and even on the toilet. Each killing had been precise and gruesome, with a single shot between the eyes, to blow out the back of the head, and a second through the chest, to shred the heart into bits. Every victim had a piece of paper crumpled inside their mouths with a catchphrase meant to be funny. *Didn't see that coming, did you? Knock knock. Peekaboo. Sweet dreams. Probe this. Got toilet paper?*

The scenes angered and horrified Desmond. Many of the dead had been his friends. These were people he had worked and trained with over the years. Now, they were all dead.

When Desmond learned that his name had finally come up on the list, an image of his lifeless body flashed inside his head with a crumpled-up piece of paper crammed inside his mouth that said *Superspy no more.*

No. Not if he could help it. Not like them.

He wasn't going to sit around, hide, or wait for a bullet to hit its mark, much like his friends had. This was a game of kill or be killed, leaving him with no choice but to kill. Desmond set out on the road. His intuition led him into the southern states, and for the second time in his life, by the grace of good luck, he found TJBJ in the desert, gassing up at a truck stop.

The Superspy waited till the truck stop was empty. He took careful aim with his rocket launcher from way atop a hill one mile down the road. From his scope, he could see the relaxed expression on TJBJ's face. This man was without a care in the world. So many had died from his rifle, yet here he was sucking on a straw from his cold drink, enjoying the calming desert breeze. Desmond held his breath and took aim. He squared his shoulders and readied his finger against the trigger. He tapped it gently. In that moment, TJBJ lifted his head, like a dog sniffing the air. He turned and met Desmond's eyes. The Superspy paused. The elite sniper was known to be quick on the draw. He could easily squeeze out two precise shots from where he stood before Desmond could fire his one, even as his finger rested on the trigger. Strangely, TJBJ smiled and put the straw back inside his mouth. He turned back around and reclined against his truck, giving his back away to the Superspy. Without hesitation, Desmond pulled the trigger and watched the rocket's pulsating glow zoom across the sky into the gas pumps. The gas station exploded into a ball of fire. TJBJ's truck was hurled into the air and came crashing down like a meteor. After the fire had subsided, all that remained of the gas station was scorched metal, with the redneck's body nowhere to be found. The Agency concluded that no one could have survived such an explosion. They declared TJBJ dead and Operation Junk Food a success. Desmond was praised as a hero and rewarded with a medal of valor.

But the Superspy had pondered over the years if the elite sniper had truly been killed. The Agency had dubbed him *hard to kill* in the past. A man of his caliber and performance could very easily survive a spotted ambush. Sabio's fuzzy imagery of the man in the hat, living in middle of the woods, had finally put to rest all the contemplation. Not only was TJBJ alive and well, but he had kept himself busy. He faked his own death and hid inside Freeland, then Hidden Trails, as he planned ways of exacting revenge on the Agency in a time they least expected it.

Desmond dropped to the ground.

He had dismissed it the first time, thinking it was nothing, but it was more apparent the second time around. He listened carefully.

Twigs. Several twigs. Snapping under the pressure of heavy boots.

Desmond lessened his breaths and gripped his knife. He saw movement from the bushes up ahead. The movement then spread out in a circle, converging on top of him. He lay still, hugging the ground so tightly he had become part of it.

The group emerged in V-formation. They maneuvered around the agent, missing him by only a few feet, wearing heavy camouflage padding, armed with high-powered machine guns.

OCTO, Desmond thought at first until he recognized the insignia stitched against their shoulders. *No...not OCTO*; these were

Billy's men. They wore the image of the Bunsen Burner, the proud chosen symbol of the redneck physicist.

After the militia moved past him, Desmond pushed himself off the ground and followed quietly in tow, keeping his distance a few trees away. He trailed the medium-size force three miles into the heart of the wilderness before the team commander crouched down and raised his fist into the air. The men, including Desmond, stopped and crouched behind him.

It lay in the distance, in between thick trees, oddly shaped, and composed of tarnished metal. It was made to resemble an army barracks, using barbed wire to lay a circular foundation around its perimeter of diesel containers, caged chickens, tires, and every car part you could imagine. Rooted behind the barracks was a set of stilts extending twelve feet high into the thick branches. Whatever lay at the top of those stilts had the perfect wilderness vantage point.

The commander motioned to one of the soldiers to advance. The soldier rose from the back of the ranks and moved up quietly, aiming his rifle at a different spot every two seconds. When he neared the barbed wire, he lowered his gun and produced bolt cutters from his knapsack. It took three precise cuts to split the wires in two, clearing a direct path into the barracks. The soldier took a careful step forward, followed by a second, and then a third when he fell to his knees, striking the ground face first.

The militia heard the delayed boom from a sniper's bullet hitting its mark. They rose to their feet, readying themselves for war. The team commander raised his fist to calm everyone's nerves. His fist then exploded into a mixture of bone, blood, and fingers. His head snapped back and burst open like a piñata, spewing out brain matter. The commander's body fell lifeless. The sound of two bullets echoed like thunder. The militia unleashed their war cry. They rushed into the open, firing blindly at the barracks.

Desmond watched closely. There was no doubt in his mind that he was about to witness a re-creation of the battle at Hidden Trails.

Many fell instantly from the sound of thunder, dead before their bodies hit the ground. One soldier pulled the pin from a grenade when it exploded inside the palm of his hand from a precise gunshot, tearing his body in two. The force from another bullet was so powerful that it plowed through a soldier's abdomen, carrying his intestines across the forest and impaling them against a tree. One soldier somersaulted forward when his right leg was blown off in the midst of his charge. He fell face first onto the ground with a second bullet striking the back of his head. The remaining sheep focused their firepower on the stilts and the above tree branches in a desperate attempt to bring down the sniper from way atop. The tree branches fired back in quick succession, taking many down with precise headshots. The last remaining soldier had his arms blown off. When he tried to run away, his legs came off below the knee. All that remained was his head and torso. The soldier cried in agony and begged for mercy. The wailing stopped as soon as his head exploded from a searing bullet.

From out of nowhere came a whirlwind of air. It picked up leaves, bodies, and trees into a powerful vortex. Desmond looked up and found the wingspan of a stealth plane shadowing the area from the sun. Its gun turrets spooled into play and opened fire on the barracks, decimating everything in its line of sight. A bullet whizzed through the air like a streak of lightning, entering the cockpit and coming out the back end. The stealth plane spiraled out of control as it hit the ground and exploded into a ball of fire. The fire quickly spread through the trees, creating a wilderness inferno with ash and metal shards raining down on the area.

Through the flames emerged the wavy figure of a man sporting an off-colored white hat, sleeveless green camouflage shirt, and blue jeans, with a rifle slung over his shoulder. He walked through the fire, admiring his handiwork.

"This all you got, you little bitch?" TJBJ screamed at the top of his lungs, his voice full of redneck rhythm. "What else you got? Come on now. I'm vexing for more."

Sabio was speechless. From where he sat, it all looked like a black-and-white videogame. The dotted white shape on top of the trees had knocked over all twenty-four charging shapes effortlessly, within a matter of minutes. Then a triangular white shape came from out of nowhere and took up the entire screen. But like the running shapes, it was easily dispatched by the small, dotted one. It took a moment for it to sink in that those weren't shapes but people. And the big triangle had been a stealth plane. TJBJ had killed them all. In all the missions he had taken part in, this was the first time he had witnessed a massacre. It was all too surreal.

On the screen, Sabio took notice of the remaining glowing shape. It was slowly moving away from behind a tree. He was hoping that it was Desmond. In all the commotion, he had lost sight of him and couldn't tell who was who anymore. Sabio throttled his joystick forward to get a closer look. It had to be him!

While TJBJ continued to admire his handiwork, Desmond used the sound of fire and destruction to mask his steps. He stood only a few feet from the man he thought he'd killed years ago. Just a few more, and he was within rushing-and-tackling distance. Desmond was going to have to time this perfectly to take the man down.

Swoosh!

Desmond looked up and caught sight of Rosemarie passing over him. When he turned back, he was met with red, glowing eyes from the elite sniper. No. Those weren't red, glowing eyes. It was a laser beam pointed between his eyes. TJBJ opened fire. Desmond saw nothing but a white flash.

Chapter 8

TJBJ

It was no secret in the underworld community that TJBJ and Billy Bob Billy Jeff Jenkins hated each other. It was also no secret that the two were brothers. Their ongoing rivalry was sparked by one of life's cruelest stalemates: they were born identical twins.

The two were so perfectly alike that no one could tell them apart growing up. They sounded the same. Acted the same. Thought the same. Functioned the same. And responded to everything the same. The brothers were so equally matched that neither could outperform the other. To make matters worse, their parents couldn't tell them apart either and kept from giving them names. They simply referred to them as *Hey, you, c'mere.*

This frustrated the twins. Life was unfair. It had stripped them of any chance at creating a unique identity for themselves, and every time they looked at each other, they saw the reason why. Contempt soon grew into anger, forcing the brothers to rely on outside factors to break the cruel cycle that was their unfair lives in the hopes of establishing one brother's dominance over the other.

The first had to do with friends. *Who could get the most friends?* The competition was fierce, lasting most of their childhood, with the brothers gaining an equal number of friends: zero. By their adolescent years, sports had replaced friends. Strength and speed were natural abilities the twins possessed. Each wowed the competition at every sporting event but could do very little to best the other half, always ending in a tie. Women came into the picture with adulthood. Then quickly left. It turned out women found the brothers repulsive.

One night, while in bed, the twins shared a collective thought at exactly the same moment.

Who could kill the other first?

This placed smiles on their faces. The first to answer the question would finally put to rest a lifelong quandary.

The family feud known as the Jenkins' War began when both parents were accidentally killed when they tried to stop their sons from dueling each other. Each twin blamed the other for their deaths and vowed vengeance. The war raged on for five years, with family clans taking sides of who they felt represented the family crest best. At the height of the war, only the brothers remained, leaving behind a trail of dead kin. As was always the case, neither could best the other. That's when the Black Hand intervened.

Because of the brothers' brutality and lack of compassion toward each other, the Black Hand considered them useful. It forced them into a truce and taught them to harness their ruthless talents elsewhere. It taught one twin to excel in science and the other to be skillful behind a rifle. Over the years, the twins became proficient at killing, and this made the Black Hand extremely proud of its identical sons. To set them further apart, it gave them each a name. TJBJ is what it named the marksman, and Billy Bob Billy Jeff Jenkins, the scientist. The reasoning behind the names was unclear, and it didn't matter. The twins were overjoyed. For the first time in their lives, they held unique identities. No more confusion between the two. They were distinct, each with his own style: Billy with his science getup and TJBJ sporting his hunting gear.

Unfortunately for the brothers, the stalemate persisted. Both were good at what they did best, neither besting the other. They competed for the Black Hand's affection, but it favored them equally. The twins were frustrated, bound toward a lifetime of stalemates until the Superspy intervened. With TJBJ presumably killed by the superagent, the Black Hand was left with no choice but to favor the only living brother. Billy Bob Billy Jeff Jenkins was pleased. The stalemate was finally over. One brother had reigned supreme over the other for the very first time, and what made things sweeter was knowing that TJBJ was still alive. Billy Bob could sense his sibling's repugnant aura even from the depths of his prison cell.

Needless to say, after Billy Bob's dramatic rescue, the Black Hand was not pleased once it found out what really happened to TJBJ. It did not like being lied to. It broke the truce between the brothers and gave Billy Bob its unbiased blessing.

If Desmond wanted to find Billy Bob Billy Jeff Jenkins, then he would have to capture the supersniper. TJBJ would no doubt know the whereabouts of his evil twin. Desmond was betting everything on the strong psychic connection the two possessed.

Capture, however, was proving extremely difficult at the moment. The minute the sniper laid eyes on Desmond, he quickly opened fire, narrowly missing his head and grazing part of his left ear. Desmond had taken refuge behind a tree.

"Did that hurt, Superdick?" TJBJ mocked openly. "Stick your head out. Let me make it all better." He unleashed a wave of bullets that tore through the foundation of the tree, causing it to burst into flames. Another shot ripped through the side. The heat from the blast seared Desmond's left thigh. His teeth clenched from the pain. It was time to move. The tree was seconds away from tumbling. He took a gas grenade from his utility belt, pulled the pin, and tossed it behind him to smoke his way out. The grenade was quickly shot away into the wilderness. Desmond tossed another gas grenade. Shot away again.

"Yeeeeehhhaaaa! Like shooting squirrel," TJBJ mocked openly again.

Desmond took a deep breath and pulled the pin off his last gas grenade, keeping it close to his chest. The thick smoke hissed loudly, consuming everything near it.

TJBJ smirked and readied his aim. He chuckled. *How sweet*, he thought. *How sweet that Superdick thinks the black smoke is going to hide him from my eagle eyes.*

He anticipated the Superspy to make a run for it. As soon as he tried, he would send his body ten feet into the air from one of his custom shots.

Before the smoke hid him from view, Desmond glanced up at Sabio, through Rosemarie, and the two shared a second collective thought. Sabio understood what he needed to do. He tightened his grip on the joystick, took a sip from his root beer, and throttled down.

TJBJ recognized the swooshing sound from earlier. He looked up at the distant glow as it grew brighter and brighter.

Rosemarie unleashed two rockets. The redneck sniper took aim and with two pulls from the trigger caused the rockets to explode in midair. Rosemarie responded with two more that were easily taken down again by sniper fire. With nothing left in its arsenal, Rosemarie nose-dived toward the sniper, who took careful aim and waited for the wind to die down before pulling the trigger.

Sabio's screen went blank. The tech wizard bowed his head and sighed with a heavy heart. Rosemarie had been his favorite; she was gone. He was also out of root beer.

The midair fiery explosion was another cause for celebration in a day filled with explosions and dismemberments. The redneck marksman couldn't remember the last time he'd had so much fun. TJBJ took a minute to marvel at his own greatness. When he was done, he turned his attention back to the Superspy and noticed a small canister rolling up to his feet. It stopped.

Bang!

The marksman dropped his rifle. He was blind. Things had become a blurry mixture of reds, yellows, oranges, and greens. He blinked repeatedly, but when that did nothing, he rubbed his eyes frantically to remove the glare. After a moment, the blurriness began to take on familiar shapes. He could make out smoke, fire, burning trees, and a running shape leaping into the air. TJBJ fell to the ground when the kick connected against his chest, knocking his hat off. He frantically felt the ground for his rifle. When his fingers felt cold steel, he stood back up, firing blindly into the surrounding flames. His face suffered a right cross as a result, followed by an uppercut that caused him drop his rifle again. TJBJ took a step back and clamped his eyes shut. He shook his head violently to rid himself of the cobwebs stuck inside his head. When he opened his eyes, things were clear again. The sniper extraordinaire gazed at the Superspy with a pair of unblinking, devilish eyes. He reached down, picked up his hat, and snugged it back on top of his head. He cracked his knuckles with a full-on smile.

Game on.

The two circled each other for the second time in their fighting careers, with the burning forest as their backdrop. They sized each other up: TJBJ with that disgusting grin on his face and Desmond with his look of determination. Ashes rained down on the men as the two engaged with the lighting speed that one would expect from two extraordinary adversaries. Punches, kicks, and elbows were thrown, with Desmond gaining the advantage. Finally, they clinched. TJBJ's brute strength proved too much for the Superspy, and Desmond felt his body move backward through fire and into the burning bunker till he was pinned helplessly against the wall.

"Looks like I got you pinned, Superdick." A wave of awful breath spewed from TJBJ's mouth, showcasing his yellow, crooked teeth caked in cavities.

Desmond turned away in disgust. "Brush your teeth."

"I will—soon after I kill you. I think I'll use one of your fingers as a toothbrush. What do you think about that?"

Desmond kicked off the wall. "I...don't...think...so." He pushed TJBJ across the bunker, pinning him against the opposite end.

"Yeah! Yeah! I like it when my prey fights back. Makes them think they have hope." TJBJ kicked off the wall with all his strength.

"But...they...don't." He pushed Desmond back against the opposite wall, which knocked the wind out of him. "I've been waiting a long time for this." Saliva drooled from his mouth, like a wolf savoring its kill. "You think I forgot what you all did to me? All that anal probing."

Desmond pushed off again and pinned TJBJ against the opposite wall for the second time. "The Agency wanted to know what hillbilly rednecks with good marksmanship ate. It was science."

TJBJ pushed him against the opposite wall. "*Science?* I told them what I ate! Possum, squirrel, run-over squirrel, run-over possum—but they kept on drilling, looking for gold. Even after I told them how much I loved Mexican food."

Desmond pushed TJBJ against the opposite wall a third time. "You've never had real Mexican food."

TJBJ pushed Desmond back into the opposite wall. "Don't tell me I ain't never had it. I hate people who tell me I ain't never had it. I've had it all! Nothing but the best. Cletus's Mexican possum bonanza and Floyd's alligator enchiladas. You telling me that ain't authentic?

"No! No one's ever heard of any of it. It's time to wake up and face the truth TJBJ."

"And what's that?"

"That you've never had a taste, a nibble, a licking of authentic Mexican food. Never. Not in your *whole* life."

TJBJ lost it. He screamed and pushed Desmond to the ground. The Superspy reached back and pulled out the semiautomatic pistol strapped to his back. He took aim, but TJBJ slapped it out of his hand. The elite sniper pulled out a shotgun from out of nowhere. He aimed. Desmond froze. He pulled the trigger. Misfire. Desmond snatched the barrel away and stood back up. TJBJ took a swing, but Desmond ducked and felt the Superspy inside him come alive. With all his might, he released a roundhouse kick that knocked the sniper completely out, sending his face into the ground.

It was late in the evening when TJBJ woke up and found himself inside his burned-out bunker. He noticed the fire was out, leaving the forest a charcoal black with a heavy mist of ash in the air. He tried to stand but couldn't. He was tied to a chair. He laughed. It was a dark, sinister, maniacal laugh—the kind that bad guys in the movies love to show off. He kept laughing till water was splashed all over his face.

A few feet away were the Superspy and Sabio, glaring down at him with interrogation lights booming to life from both ends.

TJBJ started with his sinister laugh again. He found his predicament hilarious. Sabio splashed another bucket of water onto the madman's face.

"You quit splashing water on me!"

"Stop laughing, and I will." Sabio refilled the bucket. "You give me the creeps when you laugh like that."

"Where is he?" Desmond's eyes were cold, and his voice was serious.

"Where is who?"

"Don't play dumb."

"Oh, so that's what this is all about. Billy Bob escaped, and you need my help." He smiled, and there he went again with the laughter until Sabio splashed him with another bucket of water. TJBJ shook the wetness off like a wet dog. "If I ever get out of this, I swear I'll—"

"Where is he!" Desmond interrupted, his voice louder this time.

"I don't know. And even if I did, I wouldn't help you."

"Not even after he tried to kill you?" Sabio asked, bringing to light the destructive incident from a few hours ago, caused by his own twin brother.

"No."

"What about the Black Hand?" Another fact brought to light, this time by Desmond.

TJBJ said nothing.

"It's only a matter of time before it finds you. We can help. Keep you safe."

"I see what you're doing. You're both trying to trick me. Get all me scared so I tell you what you want to hear. Well, it ain't gonna work. I ain't saying anything. Not a single word. You hear me? Nothing. Not for all the donkey-grilled Mexican burritos in the world."

"That's not even Mexican food," Sabio said, confused. "You just don't get it, do you?"

"Maybe it's you who don't get it, chubby. Maybe it's both of you who don't get it."

Desmond flipped the chair over. TJBJ grunted as his face hit the floor. He spat out blood and smirked at the Superspy. "Is that all you got, Superdick?"

That's when he heard it. That all-too-familiar buzzing sound he'd endured for weeks while in the hands of the Agency. TJBJ looked in horror at the cylindrical spinning object in Sabio's hand. It resembled a hand drill, with a smooth, metallic, chrome arrowhead tip.

"Turns out the past findings of your diet were inconclusive," Desmond informed him. "The Agency has asked for more tests." Desmond nodded at Sabio.

"Wait…wait!" TJBJ cried out.

Desmond pulled down TJBJ's pants. Sabio drew closer with the probe and began lubricating the tip with Vaseline.

"I said wait, dammit! Wait! Slow your role! Slow your role! I don't know where he is."

"I don't believe you." Desmond pulled down TJBJ's boxer shorts. "If he knows where you are, then you must know where he is. You two are in sync."

"Not always. And really, how hard was it to find me? I'm the only goddamn redneck in the whole United States that loves Mexican food, living in the middle of absolute nowhere. A child using the Internet could find me. You two should be ashamed at calling yourselves spies."

The anal probe stopped spinning, and both Sabio and Desmond shared a look. "He is kind of right," Sabio agreed.

"I don't care. Probe him."

The probe spun back to life. TJBJ grew frantic and desperate. "Check my momma's house. He always goes there."

"We did. He ain't there." Sabio positioned himself behind TJBJ.

"The basement, then."

"We did that too. Want to spread those butt cheeks for me, Superspy?"

"Happy to." Desmond slapped on a pair of rubber gloves. "Stop pinching them, TJBJ. Don't make this harder than it really has to be."

"Wait...wait...I lied. I'll tell you where he is...I'll tell you." TJBJ was out of breath. Sabio turned off the probe, and Desmond let go of the sniper's butt cheeks.

"The Devil's Balls. He's at the Devil's Balls. He's got a hidden base there. That's where he is. I can feel it," he said with watery eyes.

Desmond and Sabio turned and proceeded to walk out of the bunker.

"Wait. Wait!" TJBJ screamed. "You two sons of bitches aren't just gonna leave me like this?"

"Our boys will be over soon...to continue the testing," Desmond reassured him.

"What? No! Let me out! My ass can't take another drilling! It hurts when I sit!"

The dynamic duo left, but in the background they could still hear TJBJ's girly cries for mercy.

Chapter 9

The Devil's Balls

Six Huey helicopters roared through the evening sky with bellies full of heavily armed soldiers ready for war. Their destination—the Sanora Desert, spanning hundreds if not thousands of brown-orange miles bejeweled with peculiar rock creations and nocturnal wildlife across its beautiful landscape. But its true main attraction lay vastly ahead, a monumental giant that had remained dormant for millions of years. The Native Americans referred to it as *Fertile Mountain*, but the Western world came to know the geological wonder as *the Devil's Balls*.

For millions of years, the towering spectacle thrived as an active supervolcano responsible for the creation of the surrounding desert lands. When bursting magma caused the collapse of its volcanic neck, the fiery giant was finally silenced and transformed into the now-slumbering sixteen-thousand-foot spectacle. Over time, erosion had chipped soundly away at its solid form, sculpting a thick, massive, long peak flanked by two smaller, rounder peaks that gave the mountain the appearance of a fully erect penis, bursting through the earth, only to penetrate the virgin sky—a visual that could be seen clearly from space.

For hundreds of years, the Native Americans regarded the dormant superpenis as a fertility god who granted fruitfulness to those who pursued it by scaling the mountainous peak and kissing its rocky, smooth tip. In their eyes, the geological wonder was a symbol for life and eternity, imbuing the gift of soul to an otherwise semibarren, desolate land. But when Western eyes first glanced upon its awe-inspiring towering profile, they came to see it under a different filter. The supervolcano made Western men feel small. Very small. In places that mattered most. For them, life and prosperity were now things that could only be measured in inches. Inches that were severely lacking. For this reason, and this reason alone, the mountain was regarded as evil—unadulterated evil that could only stem from the very depths of evil itself, Lucifer. It was his mocking gesture to man that he would never fully rise to the occasion. So to speak. Thus, the Devil's Balls.

The helicopters circled the area, allowing several of the soldiers to take selfies with the fertile wonder in the background before it was time to get ready. They flew over the right testicle and hovered directly above the zigzagging canyons that resembled wrinkles or veins, depending on what angle you were looking at them from. The men locked, loaded, and rappelled one by one. A total of twenty landed safely on bedrock, surrounded by a whirlwind of dust stirred up by the helicopters' spinning blades. They moved down the canyon in unison. The canyon meandered in circles like a coiled-up snake before coming to a metal door. They planted explosives.

Boom!

The metal door gave way. They rushed in, descending down a metal staircase, landing on leveled cement with the air thick and heavy and the area covered by darkness. Dust particles floated freely, reflecting off the tactical lights like pixie dust, inviting the men farther down the endless corridor where several mysterious pathways lined the walls, branching off into more hidden areas. The men split up into three teams. Omega and Beta veered left and right while Alpha team remained at the forefront.

Alpha team kept their fingers ready on the triggers in case Billy Bob's men decided to stop playing hide-and-seek from out of the shadows. Their quick pace took them through the dust-layered command hub full of unused computers, the sleeping quarters swarming with overturned bed frames, and an empty mess hall with plastic trays scattered across the floor. Their pace ultimately led them straight into a warehouse. The Alpha team leader raised his fist. The men stopped as he scanned the area.

The warehouse was medium in size and mostly empty say for a few wood crates and rusty metal rods on the floor. Above them, the team's tactical lights revealed a metal catwalk that outlined the square enclosure. Alpha team had apparently come to a dead end.

"Omega, anything?" the Alpha team leader spoke into his collar radio.

"Negative, all empty."

"Beta?"

"Negative. Nothing but rats."

"Copy you," the Alpha team leader responded.

He turned to his men and removed his tactical helmet. The team knew what this meant. They lowered their guns and relaxed their postures. Some moaned in disappointment. They were all itching for a fight, but there wasn't going to be one today. From the looks of things, the base had been abandoned several years ago.

"Radio Command. Let them know that we have a false lead," the Alpha team leader instructed.

A soldier acknowledged when the wailing caught them all by surprise. Alpha team spun around, aiming their sights ten feet away. They advanced slowly. The white lights exposed sharp bones wrapped by a thin layer of wrinkled, spotted flesh. Its hands were trembling, trying to hide its face from the oncoming brightness. Its teeth were chattering but smiling. It wanted the men to come closer.

The Alpha team leader noticed the shiny object in its right trembling hand. Suddenly, its body thrashed violently. Foam discharged from its mouth. Its blue, faded eyes gazed upon the men with disgust.

Desmond entered the base an hour after the infiltration team, followed by Sabio and a few field agents. They had found the base just as the infiltration team had earlier: abandoned, with no signs of life.

"Alpha team, come in." Desmond spoke into his radio but received only static. "Beta, Omega, do you read?" More static.

They moved carefully through the corridors, continuing to call out to the teams by radio. After a mile into the complex, they grew desperate and began calling out to the men by voice and first names. No answer. The dark corridor took them through several more passageways till it led them into the warehouse. That's where they found the infiltration team. All three teams were huddled inside. Their lifeless bodies were stacked on top of each other in the shape of a pyramid with a long metal rod piercing through their flesh a la shish kabob. At the very tip of the rod was a flag with a stitched insignia they all knew too well. A Black Hand.

"What happened here?" Sabio asked, horrified by the scene.

That's when Desmond caught a glimpse of it. It was buried between the spent bullet casings. He plucked it off the floor and held it sensibly in his hand. It weighed next to nothing and dripped with green ooze.

What is this?

The hairs on the back of his neck stood up as goose bumps raced all over his flesh. His hand gripped his pistol tightly. Whatever killed the men was still inside the warehouse. He could sense it smiling. His eyes were drawn to the dark back corner. A part of him wanted to lift up his flashlight and reveal what desperately wanted to show itself. The other half was too afraid to. The Superspy within was nowhere to be felt. He was not ready for this fight.

"Let's go."

"What?" Sabio was confused. "But what about the men—"

"Go. Now!"

Desmond pushed Sabio and the agents back down the corridor. As he backpedaled through the warehouse, he kept his eyes trained on the dark corner, at the unseen smile watching him leave. As they made their first turn down the passageway, the ground shook violently from a powerful earthquake. The men were rocked to the floor.

Desmond knew that it was no earthquake. Something enormous had begun to chase after them. If they were going to survive, then they needed to move.

"Run!"

The men quickly stood up and dashed down the corridor at top speed. Desmond and the agents had taken several corners when they realized Sabio was nowhere near their pace. The chubby agent was trailing seriously behind. He was breathing heavily, with pools of sweat dripping down his face. His body was showing signs of fatigue as it started to slow down.

Desmond stopped, raced back, and took the man by his arm. He pulled and dragged him along with the rest of the team, who had no choice but to slow down for them to catch up.

"I can't...I can't do this," Sabio cried out, about to collapse.

"Yes, you can," Desmond fired back. He pulled even harder on the chubby man's arm, growing desperate and angry after every struggling breath Sabio let out.

They wouldn't be in this mess had the tech wizard not insisted on joining the infiltration group. He claimed it was his right as he was part of the team. Despite everyone's protests, Desmond allowed it, knowing he would probably regret it. He was definitely regretting it now. All he wanted to do was show Sabio how out of his element he was, and that he could not maintain his own because he was not a field agent. His function was to lend support. That's all!

Sabio was probably realizing that now—only now was going to get everyone killed. Thoughts of letting go of Sabio's arm came to Desmond's mind. Perhaps it would be best to let go and leave him to fend for himself so the others could make their escape.

Desmond shook the thought away. Sabio was his partner—a rather unfortunate fact he would have to endure and see through to the end. Until then, it was his responsibly to keep him alive, along with keeping himself safe.

"The door! Close it!" Desmond shouted.

As soon as they passed through a sealable section of corridor, the agents closed and bolted the door behind them. They did this for every sealable section they passed to buy themselves some time. But it was useless. A few seconds after they sealed the door, they could hear it bursting open from the wave of brute energy chasing after them.

The corridors were now vibrating. The ceiling pipes were coming undone. The walls were sprouting cracks. *Thump...thump...thump...thump* was growing closer and closer, like the sound of war drums, looming heavy and large.

"Gas grenade," Desmond screamed over the noise. An agent tossed one over. The Superspy pulled the pin and tossed it behind him.

Poof!

Smoke took the corridor. The vibration slowed down but only by a bit. Then it resumed, building itself back up, growing stronger and stronger.

"Throw everything!" he yelled.

The agents tossed gas and flash grenades over their shoulders. As they turned the corner, they heard them exploding off the walls like firecrackers. That only seemed to piss off the charging bull. They heard a monstrous scream and felt a blast of air rush through the corridor like a gust of wind. The nameless fear charged at full speed.

Daylight!

This was it. It was now or never. A last desperate sprint. At the far end of the corridor was life. Behind them was death. A death far worse than what the infiltration team had experienced. They had to make it.

The sheer kinetic energy from the oncoming charge caused the compound to come undone. Cement chunks rained down on the men as they raced up the metal stairs. They exited the base but didn't stop there. They continued racing toward the helicopter waiting for them at the far end of the canyon. They jumped immediately on board. Sabio had to be hauled inside. Desmond raced into the cockpit.

"Go! Go! Go!" he screamed. The pilot pulled the joystick up, and the chopper lifted into the air, tumbling the men inside.

"Bomb it."

"Sir?" the pilot said, confused.

"Do it!"

"Copy. Coming around."

The pilot maneuvered the chopper around and released a fiery display of explosions onto the right testicle of the Devil's Balls, blowing away chunks of supporting rock. The mountainous penis came tumbling down on its right side, leaving behind a cloud of dust that covered the area for miles.

Desmond nodded at the pilot and gave his thumbs-up to return to base. He took his seat and strapped himself in, slowly sinking away into his thoughts.

"What did you see?" Sabio asked in between breaths.

Desmond said nothing. He wasn't sure what he'd seen. He'd never been afraid of anything his whole life. Yet when he looked into the darkness and saw evil glaring back at him, he wasn't sure what to do. Desmond noted that his hands were trembling. The strange metal syringe he'd found in the warehouse slipped from his fingers and made a loud clanking sound when it hit the floor. It rolled off the edge of the helicopter and plummeted back down to the earth.

Chapter 10

Gato Negro

Madeline resembled an airline stewardess more than a factory tour guide.

She wore a blue business suit, paired with blue heels and a white scarf, and used black eyeliner to accentuate the color in her sparkling brown eyes. Her blue scrunchie brought the look together into a tiny, cute blond bun, and this made it difficult for many not to inquire about flight departure times when they came in contact with the faux flight attendant.

Madeline didn't mind the jests. She loved her job and laughed with the rest of them. She made it a point to look professional and presentable when representing the Gato Negro brand, which in her case was all the time. When top employees were ranked, Madeline was always number one.

"Good morning!" she said with a positive blast of energy. "How are you today? I'm so happy that you are all here. We're going to have so much fun together." She laughed—more like giggled—showcasing the ultrawhites of her perfectly bleached teeth.

"My name is Madeline, and I will be your fun-loving guide." She laughed again and spoke rather quickly, running out of breath at the end of each sentence. "Welcome to the Gato Negro plant, founded by the Gonzalez family over a *hundred years ago*," she said with mystery and awe. "Now if you kindly take a step back, we can begin our tour. Please step back. Step back. Thank you."

She turned around and faced the towering nine-foot stainless-steel doors. She raised both arms into the air and spoke thunderously loud. "Open the doors."

The doors hissed. A small discharge of gas overtook the crowd unexpectedly, gaining a few jumps and laughs. With the parting of the steel doors came a reverberation that grew stronger and louder with every second that passed. A ray of light pierced through the cracked opening, overtaking the twenty-one tourists, who quickly shunned away. As the sound grew louder and stronger, the doors arrived at their limit and locked themselves in place through an unseen mechanism lining the inner walls that echoed a thundering boom. A wave of *oooohhh*s and *aaaahhh*s came from the crowd with the dimming of the blinding light, exposing the monstrous inner workings of the plant, like the inside of a giant's intestines. The crowd took to their cameras, but before they could click away, Madeline stood before their lenses and raised her hands to keep the crowd in order.

"Please. Please. There will be plenty of time to take pictures. Right now, I need everyone to line up and stay inside the yellow pedestrian lane, or as I like to call it, the *yellow brick road*." The crowd laughed. "It has been placed there with your safety in mind, and I cannot begin the tour until everyone is in place. Is everyone in place? Are we good? *Super.* Everyone, follow me and stay close."

The yellow brick road led the group through sections of the plant like a game of Pac-Man. It took them under, over, and around machinery that boasted the advancements in plant engineering.

For the tourists, there was no denying the facility's magnificence. It was as sterile as a hospital and as wide and deep as an airport, composed entirely of stainless steel vats, gears, pumps, suction devices, conveyor belts, mainframes, and zigzagging cranes that rolled across the open space via ceiling tracks. The most striking detail came from the lack of human interaction. There wasn't a single human being on the factory floor with the exception of the tourists.

Madeline brought the crowd before a row of shuddering vats that were in the middle of the mixing process. "Like I stated before," she said loudly over the roar of the vats, "the Gato Negro family plant has been around for one hundred years, but its sauces have been around for over two hundred years."

Someone in the group whistled; a few took pictures of the moment.

"Yes, no joke. Two hundred years," she continued. "Two hundred and one this August."

"How is that even possible?" a curious voice from the crowd spoke out.

"That is a very good question with an answer that I don't have, unfortunately." Madeline pouted. "Even after working here for ten years, there are still things about the Gato Negro plant that even I don't know. But from what I've been told, it's a secret the company holds dear to its heart." She giggled.

The same voice spoke out a second time. "Where are all the people?"

"Another good question and one that I was getting to. As you all know, Gato Negro has many sauces in its product line with the delicious, mouthwatering, ever-craving Agua Dulce BBQ sauce as the flagship product. It's been named the preferred BBQ sauce of choice from restaurants and steakhouses around the country. And"—she paused for effect—"the main export of choice from around the world." The crowd was impressed. "Some say you could put it on just about anything deep fried, grilled, or even raw, and it will still taste *muy delicioso*."

The crowd laughed. Madeline relished the moment. She was impressed at how good her Spanish was getting.

The voice spoke a third time. "Why are there no people?"

"I was getting to that, sir. If you could kindly be more patient." Madeline peered into the crowd to see who the voice was coming from, with no luck.

"In order to preserve the secret recipe, the Gonzalez family decided to let *machines* do all the work," she said in awe. "That's right. *Machines* do all the work here. Not people. As of right now, *we* are the only human beings on the factory floor."

The group was impressed. A few nodded; others took pictures of the vats, computers, and factory floor to commemorate the valuable insight.

"This way, please."

Madeline led the group away from the rattling sounds and into a quiet, soundproof, sterile, white room. She invited everyone to join her by her side. "This is where all the prep work takes place. Now, watch carefully," she said with a grin full of excitement.

Fruits, vegetables, meats, and an assortment of exotic spices were brought in from a conveyor belt that traversed the medium size space. It dumped the ingredients onto a table three-quarters the size of the room. From the ceiling came an army of mechanical arms wielding sharp knives. They took their place around the table and with lightning speed chopped with such ferocity that many in the group became instantly entranced by the ensuing chaos and took pictures. Others took a step back, a bit frightened of the chopping spectacle. In the end, the scene was a bit too much for everyone. The tourists kept a safe distance against the back wall and looked away. The only one enjoying the chopping bonanza was Madeline. She watched with wild eyes, savoring the high intensity of the shimmering blades. She laughed hysterically and turned to the crowd with a feverish smile, hoping they felt the same way she did at the moment.

"Isn't it amazing?" she said as fruit juices and meat sauce freckled her smiling face like specks of blood.

After the blades finished slicing and dicing, more mechanical arms came to mix the ingredients into a large bowl.

"Is that the real reason why people aren't allowed inside the plant? Because it's dangerous?" That same voice from before spoke out for the fourth time.

"No, that's not the reason, sir!" Madeline was now upset. She had been robbed of her daily high.

"This whole place looks dangerous to me. I would think that's the real reason why no people are allowed."

"Well, it's not, whoever you are." She looked into the crowd, still not sure who the interrupter was. "Why don't you come out and show yourself?" she demanded.

The crowd looked among themselves and weren't quite sure who was speaking. The voice had gone silent.

The end of the tour brought the tourists into the loading area, where miles upon miles of conveyor belts were used to move glass bottles. The bottles were then packaged into boxes by actual people dressed in hazmat suits. Lastly, the boxes were loaded into the back of semitrucks.

"This is the only time that people come into the process." Madeline made the announcement as the group watched truck drivers close and lock their back doors before driving off onto the highway. "Their jobs are as important as the machines'. They package and load the product to be trucked away by highway so it can arrive safely at your favorite restaurants and into your favorite meals." She turned to the crowd and smiled. "In summation, Gato Negro is the world's leading BBQ sauce exporter. We ship twenty-four hours a day, seven days a week to anywhere and everywhere in the world. We never stop producing for anything or anyone."

She paused. Something caught her attention. She turned to the crowd and urged everyone to come closer till the tourists were huddled around her.

"As you all know, Mr. Gonzalez, the current owner of Gato Negro, is a very busy man," she said in a whisper. "He's never around because he's always traveling the world on business. But if you look behind me…you might just get a little surprise."

The crowd raised their heads and saw a five-foot-seven, heavyset Mexican, wearing a black business suit, crossing the factory floor. He was surrounded by an entourage of men, also wearing black suits, who surveyed the area carefully and were never too far away from their employer.

The crowd quickly took photographs. The flashes of light caused Roberto Gonzalez to pause. His men reached inside their jackets. Roberto quickly held them back. The word *turistas* was heard.

"If you all wave, we might just be lucky enough to get him to wave back." Madeline waved. The crowd mimicked the happy-go-lucky tour guide.

Roberto Gonzalez waved and smiled in return.

"Yay!" Madeline and the tourists clapped. They took more pictures of Roberto Gonzalez as he disappeared into the back offices, followed by his men.

"Well." Madeline clasped her hands together. "I hope you all enjoyed the factory tour. And I hope that I was, to some degree, satisfactory to your liking."

The crowed chuckled.

"There is a survey that I would kindly appreciate if you would all fill out. You can find it in the gift shop, where we have prepared a lunch platter for you to sample our finest BBQ sauce!" she said excitedly.

The group cheered.

The tourists followed Madeline into the gift shop, where the crowd spotted a platter of tender pork ribs smothered in Agua Dulce BBQ sauce in the center of the room. They ate calmly and spoke among themselves about the tour. When a second courtesy platter was brought out, they took to it like rabid animals, foregoing any small talk. The tourists fought over pieces, their faces caked in BBQ sauce as they licked their fingers feverishly clean. They demanded a third platter. It was brought out in the hopes of suppressing their appetites, but it didn't. When Madeline refused to bring out a fourth, fighting broke out among the crowd. They accused each other of eating more than their fair portions. What started out as a peaceful, loving group ended in a frenzied, fighting crowd. The gift shop was torn to bits. Security was called to break up the skirmishes, with many tourists placed in handcuffs, while others left angry when they were kicked off the premises.

"Why does it always end this way?" Madeline uttered somberly as she watched the group leave. "How many?" she asked the security guard standing next to her.

"Twenty," he said and walked away.

"Twenty," Madeline repeated the number. "*Twenty?*" she said again in confusion.

She'd counted twenty-one at the beginning of the tour. Not twenty. Come to think of it…she never found out who'd kept interrupting her tour.

Madeline returned to the gift shop and tiptoed her way through broken glass. She made her way past the double back doors and stopped short at the loading dock. She examined the workers in the hopes of spotting someone peculiar. To her disappointment, there was no one.

Chapter 11

Roberto Gonzalez

Roberto Gonzalez walked with focus and determination. His strides through the hallways were quick, leaving his men behind a trail of sparkling sweat. He had no time for them. Much like he had no time for time itself. The matter was urgent—so urgent that it was painful. So painful that it was urgent. And so urgent that it forced his teeth to gnash uncontrollably against one another from how painful the matter was. In short, Roberto Gonzalez...had to pee. After a four-hour car trek without the option to stop, a bathroom break was a desperate cry for help. This man's bladder was on the verge of exploding if immediate release wasn't attained, and soon.

In the distance, Roberto caught a hint of relief. A bathroom had appeared from out of nowhere. Finally, everything was going to be all right. The unremitting pain he had endured for so long was only ten feet away from glorious release. He could feel the pain subsiding from his body. It would all be over soon, very soon.

The destressing moment came to an abrupt halt when an office door burst open. A stranger came charging out on a head-on collision with the heavyset Mexican. Roberto stopped dead in his tracks. He was quickly swarmed by his men, who pulled out semiautomatic machine guns.

The stranger came to a squeaking stop. He raised his hands in the air.

"He's from the factory, *idiotas*." Roberto pushed through his men, annoyed at how blindsided they had become. He could clearly make out the hazmat suit that workers wore in the shipping area.

The factory worker was dragged back into the loading area while the remaining guards secured the bathroom stalls. Roberto did his rendition of the peepee dance while he waited for the signal that everything was clear. After the longest minute of his life, his guards came out and nodded at their employer.

The zipper couldn't have come off any quicker. When it finally did, he was rid of a four-hour throbbing pain that gushed out of him like Niagara Falls. He moaned in instant relief and flushed with satisfaction after five minutes. He walked calmly to the sink, washed his hands, and splashed water onto his face. When he opened his eyes, he was disturbed at the reflection staring back at him. It was tired, sporting an unshaven face, with disheveled hair and wrinkled clothes. The bags underneath the eyes showed how very little sleep he'd had in the past few days.

Roberto could not remember that last time he'd enjoyed a good night's sleep. He had been on the run ever since they came from out of the night sky. They swarmed his plantation, taking it by force. Many of his men died protecting it. Roberto watched in horror as the home his family built a hundred years ago was set on fire. Memories of his childhood, parents, grandparents, and past generations—all gone in a mixture of ash and flames. The invaders made it clear they were there for him, and they would stop at nothing until he was theirs. The intent was escalated when they threatened to kill his wife and daughter if he didn't give himself up. But Roberto was one step ahead of his would-be captors. He had evacuated his family through an underground passage that led out into the thick forest. From there, they were taken away by helicopter and flown out of the country to a house belonging to one of his investors in Cuba. They were safe for now. The same could not be said for Roberto. He loved his family too much to put them in danger. He chose not to go with them. He took to the highways with his armada of bulletproof jeeps instead, ping-ponging from factory to factory, sleeping a few hours at a time till he had to move on to the next destination. The constant runaround was proving to be too much for the fifty-seven-year-old. He needed to rest. But his would-be captors weren't resting. They seized every production plant they came in contact with in their search for Roberto. They robbed him of all transported goods, including those destined for the oversea markets. If they couldn't have him, then they would chip soundly away at the legacy his family created over a century ago.

The only option left was to give himself up. That would halt the madness and restore everything back to the way it had been. He would get to see his family again.

Roberto slammed his fist on the sink.

No, it wouldn't!

There were no guarantees they would stop. They were bent on destroying him. This wasn't part of the deal. It had never been discussed. No one said secrets had to be revealed.

Why? Why was this happening?

Roberto had seen enough. He turned away from the mirror, sickened by the sight of the pathetic, restless man. He made for the exit when he noticed the stranger blocking it. He was dark skinned and medium height, wearing khaki-brown shorts, flip-flops, and a Hawaiian shirt with a camera hanging from around his neck. Beneath his feet lay the ceiling panels the stranger had apparently broken through.

"For an *asesino*, chu are very funnie looking," Roberto said with his thick Mexican accent that mixed and played with English words.

"I'm from the Agency," the stranger said in a deep voice.

"Whish agency?"

"Thee Agency."

"There are many agencies."

"I'm from the one that counts," the stranger said, sounding sure of himself.

"Well, let's see. There's the Agency of Cruelty to Animals. That one counts. There's also the Agency of Foreign Affairs. That one counts also. The Agency of Marital Affairs. The Agency of Chupacabras—"

"I'm from...*the*...Agency." The stranger shared a look with Roberto. They suddenly understood one another.

"Ohhhhhh. *La Agencia*," Roberto whispered in Spanish. He snagged a towelette from the dispenser and wiped his hands dry. "What can Roberto Gonzalez do for...*la Agencia*?"

"You can answer a few questions."

"If chu have questions, then please take my factory tour. I'm shure Madeline can answer all of chore questions."

"I did. She left me with more questions."

"Such as?"

"Why machines? Why not people?"

"Too much overhead. I can make more *dinero* by using macheens. They don't need time off. They don't need raises. They don't get injured. They don't complain. And they don't eat."

"Machines break down. They require round-the-clock maintenance. That means you would still need people around. What's the real reason, Roberto?"

The stranger was serious. This made Roberto laugh. "*Contaminación*," he fired back.

"What contamination?"

"People. *La gente*. Everyching is automated for fear of *contaminación* by *la gente*. No human touch or presence whatsoever until the sweet BBQ sauce enters chur fragile virgin mouths."

"Then why allow tourists inside? That would put your product at risk."

"Publicity. The process is protected by the macheens. Tourists are no threat. They are chust watching."

"What can you tell me about the sauce?

"Whish one?"

"The popular one."

"There are many popular ones. Let's see…there's—"

"Agua Dulce," the stranger quickly blurted out.

"Ah, ches. Agua Dulce," he reminisced. "Ancient. Mysterious. The recipe was found on the sarcophagus of my Mayan ancestor. He was a great tribal chief."

Roberto Gonzalez pointed to the mural tile behind the stranger that was directly above the trash can. It was of a great Mayan chief standing proud, looking into the distance.

"The sauce has been in my Mayan ancestry for thousands of *años*…years. We still can't explain what it does, other than that it does it so well."

"And what is it…that it does so well?" the stranger asked, waiting intently for the answer.

"Taste *muy, muy delicioso*." Roberto smiled. "Now, please…let us cut to the chase, like a warm knife through rich, delicate Mexican cheese. Why are chu here?"

"We know that you're in hiding. We know you've been on the run for three days. We also know that your family is in Cuba, worried sick, thinking the worst has happened to you. It was by luck that I traced you here. But if I was able to find you, then that means *they* are not far behind."

"I think chu are mistaken about me. I fear no one. I have no reason to hide," he lied.

"Shipments of your sauces have been getting hijacked all over the world. We've estimated that you are losing eight hundred thousand dollars in product every day. Why allow it if you have no reasons to fear or hide?"

Roberto said nothing.

"We can help you. We can keep you safe and reunite you with your family."

"*We?*"

"The Agency."

"And how can *la Agencia* help Roberto Gonzalez?"

"We know who is responsible for all the thefts. We believe he's after the recipe to Agua Dulce. If he can't discover it by confiscating your sauce, then he'll go after the next best thing: *you*—which is why you're in hiding. We know he tried to kidnap you at your plantation. And from the looks of it, you barely managed to escape."

The stranger's reference to Roberto's survival reminded him of how unkempt his appearance was. In response, he buttoned up his shirt and slicked his hair back.

"And tell me," he said while fixing his tie, "why would such a dangerous *cabrón* go through so much trouble to discover my recipe?"

"We don't know. We were hoping you would tell us."

Roberto paused for a moment. "I haven't the slightest clue." He smirked. The glint from his perfectly white teeth told a different story. "How much?"

"For?" the stranger asked.

"How much do chu need to make this *loco* go away?"

"We don't need your money."

"I like this deal already," he said, smiling.

"We just need the recipe to Agua Dulce."

Roberto laughed quaintly. "I'm sorry. It seems that…in my old age, my hearing has gotten worse. It almost sounded like chu asked me for my *familias* thousand-year-old secret recipe. Now, what was it that chu needed?"

"The recipe to Agua Dulce," the stranger responded, with the same intensity he'd had a moment ago.

"Do you understand what chu are asking me to do?" Roberto pulled out a switchblade, unbuttoned his dress shirt, and pointed the blade at his chest. "You are asking me to cut out my heart and serve it to you in an ancient Mayan dish. Is that what chu are asking me to do?"

"That's not what I'm asking," the stranger argued.

"OK, good." He put the switchblade away.

"I'm asking for the recipe to Agua Dulce."

Roberto laughed and muttered something in Spanish. "Sorry, Mr. *Agency*, but I cannot help chu." Roberto tossed the towelette into the trash can as he made his way to the exit.

"There's a redneck mad scientist threatening to blow up the world, and the only thing that could potentially stop him is the recipe to your BBQ sauce. Can you honestly walk away, knowing that you can prevent the fiery deaths of millions and millions of people?"

Roberto stopped and met the stranger's distressed eyes. "I would rather wash the world burn in the flames of hell a million times over than give up my *familias* secret recipe. And if people are burned to a crisp, like chu say, then I'm shure they will taste good in my BBQ sauce."

"I'm afraid I must insist." The stranger was serious.

"And I'm afraid that chu are in no position to insist," Roberto answered back.

"I'm afraid I must insist that *I am* in a position to insist."

"Then I'm afraid I must insist that chu are in *no* position to insist." He snapped his fingers.

Roberto's men came charging in as thick black smoke took over the bathroom. The men quickly surrounded Roberto and waited for the smoke to clear. To Roberto's amazement, the stranger had disappeared along with the smoke.

Chapter 12

The Great Feast

The boy knew better than to have the door completely open. He held it in place with his tiny hands, supported by the door chain, leaving a two-inch gap between him and the fat stranger. His young developing mind could not comprehend any of the unspeakable acts he'd witnessed in his neighborhood growing up, and for that reason he was always on alert, distrusting of everyone.

"I'm looking for Humberto Diaz," the stranger spoke softly.

The boy's eyes grew narrowly suspicious; he was undoubtedly wondering why a fat man wearing a business suit stood outside his door, asking to speak to his father.

The fat stranger produced something from his pocket and held it for the boy to see. "I heard what happened to him. I'd like to help."

The boy stood on his tiptoes to get a peek at what the stranger possessed in his hand. It was square, shiny, the words *The Agency* reflecting brilliantly off the plastic surface. He glared at the shiny object like any eight-year-old would at a new toy. He was mesmerized by its glow, and for a brief moment, all his worries disappeared.

"Is he here?"

The stranger's question caused the light in boy's brown eyes to dim. They became suspicious again.

"I'd really like to speak with him."

Even at such a young age, the boy knew to obey the law of the neighborhood. It did not allow anyone to speak to outsiders. That's just how things worked in his big world. He knew of the consequences involved. He'd seen them scattered in the alleys, lifeless and scary. But the stranger's voice was unlike the others'. It was sincere and thoughtful. Not brutish or threatening. It wanted to help his father, who he loved so much. The boy was torn. He wasn't sure what to do except the one thing he had always done in the past when doubt crept its way into his young intuition—close the door, which he began to do slowly.

"What's your name?" the stranger asked sensibly.

This took the boy by surprise that it stopped him from closing the door. "Anthony," the boy said reluctantly.

The stranger knelt down to the Anthony's eye level and gave a comforting smile. "It's nice to meet you, Anthony. My name is Sabio. Is Humberto your dad?"

Anthony nodded.

"I'm here to help. Nothing will happen to your dad. I promise."

Anthony's eyes shifted from side to side while his young mind tried to decide what to do next. He uttered something softly.

"What was that?" Sabio asked delicately, careful not to alert or scare the boy.

"Promise?"

"Promise." Sabio extended his hand.

Anthony accepted the fat man's hand, and the two shook through the one-inch gap.

The door shut. Sabio heard the muffled sound of a chair dragged across wood floors and then bumped hard against the door. He heard Anthony grunting his way up the chair and unhooking the door chain. A second later, there was a thump followed by a delicate grunt. Anthony opened the door and held it wide open to allow Sabio's thick frame to walk inside.

"Thank you." Sabio showed his appreciation to the young lad with a slight nod and smile as he walked through. He waited for his tiny host to close, lock, and put the chain back on the door. Anthony then dragged the heavy chair back across the living room to the corner where it belonged.

"Over here," he said.

Sabio followed his young escort into the living room, where torn furniture took up most of the living space. The walls of the apartment were an off-colored white. A small TV lay center stage as the only form of light and entertainment in an otherwise bleak living space that lacked any sunlight from the windows. As they passed the kitchen, the table was full of four elderly people in the midst of a

Spanish conversation. They became frightened at the sight of the man and his business suit. Anthony spoke to them in Spanish with a calm and rational voice that seemed to ease their tension. They said nothing when he was done but watched them go into the bedroom.

"My father is right over there." Anthony pointed to the bedroom, where Sabio could see a man seated on a chair, wrapped in a thick blanket, staring out the bedroom window. "You promise to help him?" Anthony's concerned expression caused a lump to form inside Sabio's throat.

"I promise," Sabio reassured him.

Anthony smiled and raced up to his father. He whispered into his ear and then raced back into the living room to sit in front of the television to watch cartoons.

Humberto remained motionless. Whatever it was Anthony had told him had no effect. Sabio approached the man carefully, not wanting to alarm him. He laid his hand gently on Humberto's shoulder and spoke as softly as he had with Anthony. "Mr. Diaz?"

Humberto looked up with a pair of sad eyes. This man was in his midforties, with a round face and salt-and-pepper hair.

"I'm from the Agency. I'd like to talk to you about the *Great Feast*." Sabio made sure he uttered the last two words with great care.

Humberto replied with a blank stare, a response Sabio was anticipating. He was convinced that this man would deny everything.

"We're prepared to compensate you for your time."

The mention of money only seemed to amuse Humberto, who half smirked and looked back out the window.

Sabio pulled his digital recorder from his pocket and placed it on the windowsill not far from where Humberto sat. He brought over one of the chairs that was resting against the wall and took his place next to the sad-looking man who was fixated on the brick building across the street.

"Can you please tell me what happened on March 19, 2006?"

Humberto remained quiet. His interest remained on the brick building across the street.

"I understand this may be difficult for you to talk about or hard to remember, but many still don't exactly know what happened that day. As the only living witness, you're the only one who can bring out the truth."

Sabio's plea went unheard. Humberto didn't seem to care much about anything other than the brick building that blocked his view from the outside world. A prolonged bout of silence followed, and just as Sabio was about to give up, the moment was broken by the sound of Anthony's laughter. Apparently one of his favorite cartoon characters had tripped and fallen on the floor. Humberto turned and gazed affectionately at his son. Sabio took notice of this.

"Your son cares about you deeply, Mr. Diaz. He wouldn't have let me in here if he thought something bad was going to happen to you again."

Humberto looked down at the floor, considering what Sabio had just said.

"Please…let us help you by sharing your story. Do it for yourself. If not for you, then do it for your son."

213

Sabio waited patiently. The expression on the man's face had changed. The brick building had lost its enchantment. His eyes darted back and forth, lost in the past, reliving a horrific moment.

"It was Sunday," Humberto spoke slowly. "The plant was offering double time. In this town, no one turns down double time. You want to make enough money to take your family away from this place. That was always the plan." He gazed back at his son, who continued to sit still in front of the small television, drinking from a small cup of water, a big smile on his face. "So I went in."

"And where did you work?"

"The kitchen. Food prep. It was an easy job. I've done sauces all my life. Did them in Mexico and was now doing them in the United States. BBQ sauce was nothing new. I mixed by hand and cut fresh ingredients by knife. Everyone in the plant knew me as *the slicer*. No one could cut like me. I was the best." Humberto smiled for the first time since Sabio had laid eyes on him.

"Talk to me about the process."

"Like I said, we prepped and mixed everything by hand, but we were told never to touch the sauces without wearing gloves for fear of contamination. We all knew that was a lie. It had something to do with the two ingredients."

"Two ingredients?"

Humberto nodded. "They had to be mixed carefully. They brought men in hazmat suits to do it. We knew one was a chemical ingredient because the technicians told us."

"And the other?"

"A secret. We didn't know. No one knew. We called it ingredient *equis*."

"*Equis?*"

"*X*—that one came first; the chemical came last. That's how it always went."

"What went wrong that Sunday?"

"That Sunday, the mixing vats weren't working. *Nothing* was working. Our town had just experienced a hurricane that had left everything in shambles. The plant had been partially damaged, but Mr. Gonzalez wanted us to go back to work—even after the engineers had told him it was dangerous. He didn't care. He offered everyone double pay."

"I'm surprised the city didn't close it down."

"They did, at first, but Mr. Gonzalez could be very persuasive with his checkbook. He made the city look the other way while we all went back to work. Two hours into production, the pressure across the plant went crazy and caused everything to blow up. It rained BBQ sauce that morning." Humberto chuckled. "Everyone was covered in it. They all kept saying it was the best-tasting sauce they'd ever had."

"Where were you during the explosion?"

"The bathroom. I was spared from the sauce. But the chemical mixers were scared. They were screaming that everyone was covered in ingredient *equis*. They ran away. That's when the stomach pains started. Everyone was having them. They begged and screamed for help. Then they became angry and started attacking each other. That's when…"

"When what?"

"That's when…they started…to eat each other. It didn't matter if they knew the person or were family. They fed, and wouldn't stop. They came at me in the dozens. I fought them off with my knife. There were too many. I killed them…I killed many of them…they were my friends. I had no choice."

"What did the police say?"

"By the time they came, it was too late. Everyone was dead. They concluded that everyone had died from the hurricane."

"How is that possible? The hurricane happened the week before."

"Anything is possible when large sums of money are involved. The plant was officially shut down by Mr. Gonzalez and relocated elsewhere. As for me…the only surviving employee…I was laid off."

Humberto laughed.

"Can you believe it? I was laid off. I haven't been able to work since the incident. My wife left me, my parents take care of me, and my Anthony doesn't go to school. He has to work delivering newspapers to help pay rent while I sit here and waste away."

Humberto looked back out the window, angry, until he lost himself in the brick building again.

"May I?" Sabio asked, reaching for Humberto's blanket.

Humberto nodded. At this point, there was nothing left for him to hide.

With the blanket carefully removed, Sabio saw wheels, metal, and a torn cushion. It was a wheelchair, not a chair, Humberto sat on. The Great Feast had left him without the use of his arms and legs— they had been torn off and eaten by his friends on that fateful Sunday. Humberto Diaz was a head and torso only.

Chapter 13

Headquarters

"It was called the Great Feast. The story was reported by the *Santa Ana Times*, the town's only newspaper before it was shut down."

"By who?" Stencil asked curiously, not taking his eyes off the newspaper clipping he held in his hand.

"Roberto Gonzalez," Sabio responded. "You're holding the only surviving newspaper clipping reporting the incident. Thankfully, someone at the library kept a copy in case an outside source came asking about the truth. The newspaper went by eyewitness accounts from emergency crews at the scene. They were going to blow the story nationwide until Roberto purchased the paper and encouraged the staff to develop a sudden case of amnesia. Everyone was paid off except for Humberto Diaz."

"Now, why the hell would he do that? Like leaving a witness alive at the scene," Mark Stencil added.

"Roberto saw it differently. You see...this man was so grotesquely disfigured that Roberto banked on his hideous appearance to keep him from ever coming out and speaking openly about the incident. And he was right. Humberto didn't say a single word to anyone for eight years. Why pay off a man who was too ashamed and writhing with guilt over the deaths of his friends? He's blamed himself over the tragedy, not realizing it was Roberto's fault and not his."

Stencil smoothed out the curves of his handlebar mustache with his fingertips. Behind him, Central Command was still in chaos mode. Leads were rolling in hot but churning up cold nothings. Above his head, the clock was winding down, with less than twenty-three hours before Billy Bob Billy Jeff Jenkins's fat fingers hovered over his colossal red button. The Agency's only success in their desperate hunt for the mad scientist had come from three of its agents. Sabio and Desmond stood before Stencil in transmission mode, reporting on their current findings. The third agent was nowhere to be seen but no doubt listening to everything that was being said.

"We also found this." Desmond nodded at a computer jockey who, with a few clicks, brought the vid screen to life.

"What am I looking at?" Stencil asked.

"Product testing. Gato Negro files. Subject A has normal BBQ sauce."

The vid screen showed a man inside a small office, sitting behind a small table, enjoying a plate of BBQ ribs. He savored each bite and chewed leisurely, like any civilized man would if he were dining at a restaurant. He was full after one serving and thanked the scientist next to him for a wonderful meal.

"Subject B has Agua Dulce BBQ sauce."

The video switched over to a different test subject. This man was hunched over the plate, buried in BBQ ribs and sauce. He licked the plate clean when he was done and went as far as chewing on bones like a rabid animal. He demanded seconds, turning the table upside down when his request was not granted immediately. He punched several holes into the wall until a second plate was slid to him by a nervous scientist. Quickly, the test subject jumped on the tray. Then he went after the scientist.

"Holy heaven's shit!" Stencil was in shock.

"It's that addictive," Sabio noted. "The most addicting BBQ sauce ever made. Some studies have compared its addictive nature to a drug."

"With at least twelve sexual homicides in relation to that sauce," Desmond added, confusing Stencil. The Superspy raised both eyebrows and gracefully humped the air.

"Oh," Stencil responded when the visual dawned on him. "Wait. Hold on. If it can bring out that sort of hunger, why isn't the sauce causing everyone to go ape bananas?"

"Axymime," Sabio responded.

"Axy what?"

"Axymime. It's a chemical suppressor that makes the sauce edible without the need to go ape crazy. Or zombie hungry."

"Then what's making them go ape bananas?"

"We don't know. Humberto called it ingredient X. So far, our scientists haven't been able to identify what ingredient X is or how it works."

"But neither has Billy Bob," Desmond chimed in. "That would explain his interest in Roberto Gonzalez. He wants the ingredient. He was first exposed to the sauce in prison. It's all he wanted to eat. He saw promise in its addictive nature. If we can discover ingredient X before him, then we can set a trap to lure him out. Luckily for us, we know where Roberto Gonzalez is."

"We just need the green light, chief," Sabio stated, ending their report.

Mark Stencil became quiet. He wasn't the type of man who liked to rush into decisions without giving them some serious thought. Quick decisions got people killed. Desmond and Sabio knew this about the man. These moments usually took an hour or two to conclude—sometimes days. But the agents were in a desperate hurry. There was no telling how much longer they had before Roberto Gonzalez would go into hiding elsewhere.

"The man's a criminal, sir. He should be put away behind bars for what he's done." Sabio didn't hold back. Thoughts of Humberto and Anthony raced through his head. "Just give us the go, and we'll take care of it."

Stencil said nothing and curled up both ends of his mustache with his fingertips. His mind still lingered over his decision.

"Chief." It was Desmond's turn to interrupt the pensive moment.

Stencil looked up at the Superspy's blue hologram.

"Billy Bob plans to weaponize ingredient X. What we just saw was product testing at a tamed level. Imagine what will happen if it's released to the public in raw batch form. It would be a second Great

Feast but on a nationwide scale—unless we put an end to it. With less than twenty-three hours remaining, we have to move now."

Stencil's eyes fell on the clock above. The seconds were counting down quickly. He sighed heavily. He understood what was at stake.

"OK. You two are authorized to capture Roberto Gonzalez by any means necessary."

Desmond and Sabio breathed sighs of relief.

"But on one condition," Stencil added. "You two won't go at it alone."

The two agents moaned in disappointment.

"C'mon, chief."

"Yeah, we got this."

"We?" Desmond turned to Sabio, a confused expression all over his face.

"Yeah, we," Sabio responded sharply.

"*We* don't got this...*I* got this."

"*We* got this! We're a team, remember?"

"I work alone. I told you that, *remember*? You just get in the way. It's what you've been good at."

"That's not true!"

"You almost got us killed the last time."

"I saved your ass from TJBJ."

"*I* got this, chief."

"No, *we* got this, chief."

"None of you *got this*!" Stencil interrupted their bickering with his booming voice. The two men became instantly quiet. "The last time you two thought you *had this*, you ended up defacing a historical desert monument that used to be known as the Devil's Balls."

"Limp Mountain."

"What?"

"They're calling it Limp Mountain now," Sabio informed Stencil.

"Whatever. The point is you two need an escort. You're supposed to be working as a team, not bickering at each other. The Agency put the two of you together because of your strengths, and I highly suggest you put those strengths into play. Until then, I plan to send along the agent responsible for your current findings."

The news took Sabio and Desmond by surprise.

"While the both of you were busy anal probing TJBJ, she was hot on the heels of Roberto Gonzalez. If it weren't for her, we wouldn't have this lead."

"Her?" Sabio asked curiously.

"Yes, *her*. And you're going to need *her*. Roberto Gonzalez has an army. He employs Mexican day laborers."

"Is that a lot?" Desmond asked.

"If the zombie apocalypse ever happened, Mexican day laborers would outnumber them five to one," Sabio pointed out.

"Damn." Desmond was impressed.

"You'll be fine. She's good," Stencil continued.

"How good?" Desmond was curious.

"Enter," Stencil called out.

A pair of long legs, firm butt, slim waist, even-sized chest, straight black hair with a silver streak, and fair, light skin bound in black, shiny leather materialized. This woman was sexy as hell.

"Really good," Stencil concluded. "Everyone, meet Silver Fox."

"Hi, boys." She smiled.

Sabio's jaw dropped. Desmond quickly sat down on a chair and placed both hands on his lap.

Chapter 14

Ingredient X

From where Silver Fox lay, the Gato Negro plant was a blur of colored dots in the desert night three miles away. When she looked through her high-powered scope, she could make out the plant more clearly: spotlights, guard towers, barbed wire, guard dogs, and patrolling jeeps. There was an impressive amount of weaponry on display—one that you would find on a military base and not at a BBQ sauce manufacturing plant.

It was clear that Roberto Gonzalez was making a stand. He wasn't going to be captured that easily, and anyone who tried would undergo a full-on assault from his heavily armed and capable militia of Mexican day laborers who cleaned the factory floors by day but were fearsome soldiers by night. His ballsy statement, however, was also a foolish one. It painted a highly fortified "*X* marks the spot." One look at the plant and its twenty-four-story black tower, and you knew where to find the eccentric BBQ sauce man.

"Silver Fox, you read?"

Silver Fox aimed her scope into the night sky and switched over to night vision. She could clearly make out a white triangular shape gliding effortlessly through the starry night. She pressed gently on the transmitter wrapped around her neck.

"I see you, Super," she said in a sweet southern accent that could melt men's hearts instantly.

Sabio had become enslaved to it. Every sweet syllable she let loose tingled the long, untrimmed hairs in his nose and ears. He was lucky to be lying next to her as her spotter. He was even luckier to have one hell of a view: luscious lips, long black hair, toned curves, hips, and let's not forget those magnificent long, sexy legs.

"Hey, Star Trek!"

Sabio snapped out of his trance.

"Eyes out there. I need you ready."

"Yes, ma'am."

Silver Fox turned back to Desmond. "ETA, Super?"

"ETA five seconds," Desmond's voice confirmed.

Silver Fox positioned herself on the ground, lying flat on her stomach, her legs wide apart, with her high-powered EMZ sniper rifle mounted on a tripod. She pressed her right eye firmly against the scope, closing her left.

"You ready?" she asked Sabio, who positioned himself next to her, watching from his night-vision goggles.

"Yeah," he said and then took one last peek at Silver Fox's nicely toned buttocks: two sensational glowing leather lumps from the moonlight above.

Desmond swooped across the factory perimeter. From high above he could make out over two dozen patrols, giving little to no landing room. After his first sweep, he tilted up into the night sky, coming back around for another go. With his altitude steadily decreasing, he wasn't going to have enough height to bank around a third try. He needed to find a landing space, and fast.

Not far up ahead stood a single guard up against a makeshift barrack, puffing on a cigarette. This was his chance. Desmond pounded on his chest, hitting the safety release. His body dropped nine stories fast, leaving the glider to continue into darkness. The secret agent hit the ground hard, grunting into a forward roll. The guard turned around and dropped his cigarette after one look at the decked-out black shape. The guard went for his gun. Desmond quickly rushed him, knocking the gun out of his hand, and then spun him around and secured a choke hold. He wrapped his legs around the guard's waist, forcing him to the ground. The guard's body thrashed. His legs kicked everywhere. His movements lessened as the oxygen left his body and left him unconscious. Desmond released his grip and hid the body in the shadows. He crouched his way around the barracks with his tranquilizer gun at the ready. He was careful not to get in the way of any zigzagging spotlights.

"I'm in. Moving up," he said quietly into his transmitter.

"Copy," Silver Fox acknowledged.

Desmond moved vigilantly through the grounds. When guards weren't looking, he raced past them quickly. When they stood in his way, he'd find something to throw and distract them with before making a dash. He crawled when there were too many patrols and waited patiently for patrolling jeeps to pass before sprinting toward the black tower. Desmond was out of breath when he came to rest against the east guard tower. He needed a moment to recharge.

Click!

A rifle's barrel found its mark on Desmond's head. It was too late for the agent to react. The guard's trigger finger was about to pull when something whizzed through the air.

Smack!

The soldier fell to the ground with a tranquilizer round embedded deep into his neck.

"That's one," Silver Fox crackled into his ear.

"Thank you." The Superspy breathed a sigh of relief.

Desmond wasn't accustomed to thanking anyone. Nor was he accustomed to working with anyone else. Most of his missions were solo, mostly about him versus the evil underground world. Times had changed, apparently. The underground world was more dangerous with the Black Hand's return. With the introduction of Sabio and now Silver Fox, the Agency's working dynamic had also evolved. Teamwork was an idea that Desmond was going to have to get used to. And it was one that Stencil and the Agency made clear he would have to learn quickly. The Silver Fox was the Agency's best sniper, the answer to the Black Hand's TJBJ. She was undoubtedly the sexiest agent in the roster but also one of the best trackers. She can find anyone and uncover any lead. She followed through with every word and never missed a shot. With her watching his back and Sabio's navigational know-how of getting out of dangerous situations, Desmond had a chance to make it to the black tower. They had to work together.

"Sabio, lead the way. Fox, lend support."

"Copy," Silver Fox answered with a hint of gratitude. She turned away from her scope to Sabio's shocked expression. "Star Trek!" She snapped Sabio out of his trance. "You heard him. Lead the way," she said.

"OK." He nodded nervously. Sabio peered into his binoculars, still in a daze over the request. Not only had the Superspy called out for his help, but he had moved him up to team leader. Sabio wasn't sure how to respond to any of it.

"Su-Super." He cleared his throat. "Two clicks up, on my go. Fox, get ready."

Silver Fox smirked and pressed her eye against her scope. "I'm ready."

"Go!"

Desmond moved up and saw two guards walking toward him. As quickly as he saw them, they went down. He jumped over their bodies and hid behind a structural beam.

"On my say, go right. Go!"

Desmond pushed himself off the beam and raced across the ground, making a slight right where he was spotted by five guards. They shouted to each other, readying their guns. Then each went down, like ducks at a shooting gallery.

A guard dog growled from out of nowhere. Desmond spun around. The dog was let go by the guard, who urged it to kill. Desmond was about to turn and run when the dog skidded across the floor from a round to its neck. Before the guard could contemplate what had happened to his dog, his legs gave way from a dart stuck deep into his forehead.

The black tower was now a few feet away.

"Stop," Sabio commanded.

Desmond stopped and hugged the steel walls.

"Two up ahead."

Desmond could hear them. He peeked around the corner and found the men laughing, enjoying a smoke. Their bodies hit the floor before they could finish their cigarettes.

"Clear."

"Roger that," the Superspy acknowledged.

Desmond circled the tower and stopped once he reached the front doors. He knelt down and reached for the lock kit attached to his utility belt when two shots tore through the metal surface. The Superspy fell backward, unsure of what just happened. Oddly enough, he watched the doors creak open. A guard emerged. Desmond aimed his gun, about to fire, when the guard collapsed from two needles sticking out of his chest.

"How the hell did you see that?"

"We switched to x-ray."

Desmond was impressed. He stood back up. "Moving in."

He cautiously opened the door while keeping his gun in front of him and then swiftly moved inside. He pressed up against the wall, sliding across till he reached the corner. He looked around the bend, only to find a deep passageway that branched out into multiple sections. At the far end were two elevator doors that led into Roberto

Gonzalez's executive offices. They were being watched by two heavily armed guards.

"I count twelve bodies."

"I only see two," Desmond said, confused, and took another peek around the corner.

"Ten more moving toward your direction."

"What do we do?"

Sabio became quiet. *What should he do?* He wasn't sure.

"Sabio?" Desmond asked again.

Sabio turned to Silver Fox for advice but found the sniper in a meditative stance with her focus and aim at the factory. She was waiting for an answer as well.

"Sabio?" Desmond whispered a second time.

The answer became obvious at that moment. The answer had always been obvious. It had always been teamwork.

"You take the two…we'll take the rest."

"What?" Desmond was reluctant.

Silver Fox smirked.

"On my go."

"Hold up. Maybe we should wait a little bit."

"You'll be fine."

"But—"

"Trust us."

"Just give it a minute—"

"Go!"

Desmond turned the corner and raced toward the elevator. The guards saw him and took aim. Desmond fired first, striking one in the chest—he collapsed immediately. The second guard managed to squeeze off a round but missed. Desmond fired again, hitting the guard point blank in the head; he collapsed. By now, several guards had come racing from around the corner after hearing gunfire. They were converging on Desmond, leaving him nowhere to go. Then, in an awesome display of marksmanship, the walls exploded into a blizzard of tile and drywall. Desmond continued to run as everything around him exploded into millions of particles. When he reached the elevator doors, he turned, took aim, and became astonished. Every guard had been laid out from tranquilizer rounds.

He heard Sabio's voice crackle into his ear. "Clear."

"Clear," he acknowledged and then took a deep breath. Desmond pushed the elevator button. The floor indicator lit up with numbers decreasing from the twenty-fourth floor.

"Something's blocking my x-ray," Sabio said. "I can't see the top floors. Fox?"

"Same. *Trap?*" she asked, already knowing the answer.

"No doubt," Desmond acknowledged.

Ding!

The doors opened, revealing an empty square space. Desmond walked inside, cautiously checking its corners. No one was inside. He pressed the elevator button. The doors closed. He felt a slight vibration, followed by the ascent. The numbers on the panel grew steadily.

"G...od...lu...k...s...r" was the last transition he received from Sabio before everything turned to static.

Ding!

The elevator came to an abrupt stop. The doors parted leisurely to a passageway adorned with statuettes, paintings, vases, and red-carpet flooring. The ceiling was made up entirely of gold etchings in an effort to give the lengthy space the royal glow it was aiming for.

Desmond moved tentatively across the red carpet. Every painting he came across told the story of the Gonzalez family, from humble beginnings in the farmlands to the vast establishment of wealth in the city. The statuettes followed the family's line of male successors, coming to a conclusion with the statue of Roberto Gonzalez. There was a triumphant expression chiseled on the man's face as he looked into the coming horizon to bear witness to a bright future. A set of golden doors leading into the executive suite lay behind the statue. Desmond gripped the handle and found it unlocked.

The executive suite was jam-packed with Roberto's elite guardsmen dressed in black suits. At least thirty black suits had their sights set on the incoming Superspy. In the back, surrounded by all his men, Roberto Gonzalez sat behind a marble desk, drinking tea.

"Welcome back, Mr. Agency," Roberto said with a smile. "Kill him!"

All guns cocked instantaneously. Desmond smirked. The Superspy in him came alive.

They opened fire. The Superspy rushed forward, stopping center stage between the black suits. Despite his position, some were still foolish enough to open fire, hitting their own in the exchange. Desmond punched, kicked, tripped, head-butted, tackled, body-slammed, suplexed, and gave wedgies to several black suits. But there were too many to handle at once. His face, ribs, and stomach were constantly being tagged by punches and kicks. They opened fire when the chance presented itself, missing him by mere inches, and grazing him in some instances.

Silver Fox waited patiently. She hadn't moved an inch since Desmond went offline. Her right eye was still pressed against her scope; her index finger was ready to the pull the trigger. But she couldn't see anything—only static from the top floor. Despite how cool she looked, she was a bundle of nerves, just as Sabio was. They desperately wanted to know what was happening on the twenty-fourth floor. Sabio was about ready to scream from over anxiousness.

A black suit secured a full nelson on Desmond as another went after his rib cage with a flurry of punches. A right cross sent his head bobbling back. That's when he saw it. A left hook sent his head to the side. He saw it again. It was a black, square electronic device. Each time he was punched across the face, he was able catch sight of another black device on the opposite end of the room. That brought the total to three. An uppercut helped him see the fourth mounted in the opposite corner.

Desmond took a step back with his right foot and flipped over the black suit from behind. He grabbed hold of his pistol and fired at one of the electronic devices.

Sabio and Silver Fox saw a glimpse of bodies, but the visual was quick.

A black suit fired at Desmond. The Superspy dashed left and wrapped his arms around his gun, aiming it upward and shooting down another black device.

The room fizzled again. Silver Fox quickly detached her rifle from the tripod, stood up, and took aim. She was getting ready.

Desmond punched and then kicked one of Roberto's men hard in the chest, sending him flying into the arms of several others. Dazed and confused, the Superspy spun around, not sure which corner was next. He saw the ghosting image of the device on the corner ceiling and fired. Several black suits rushed him, tackling him to the floor.

Static shapes were racing across the floor. Silver Fox pulled on Sabio's collar and forced the pudgy man to his feet. She positioned him directly in front of her, resting the barrel of her rifle on top of his shoulder.

"Don't move," she told him in a cold voice, lacking the southern charm that aroused him earlier. She was dead focused on the building three miles down the road.

The black suits had Desmond pinned to the floor as he fought back, forcing the fifteen men to push back even harder. They punched, kicked, and even bit into his leg. Desmond screamed. More bodies swarmed on top of the pile, squeezing the life out of the agent's lungs. Desmond freed his right arm, aimed at the last remaining black device, and pulled the trigger. The device exploded into a thousand sparkling fragments. The walls burst open for the second time. The rounds sent men flying across the room; they struck heads, necks, chests, buttocks, and groins with such accuracy that they sent the men fleeing for the exit.

Silver Fox fired furiously into the room. Sabio stood still, blinded by the white muzzle flashes from the sniper rifle.

"Reload," she screamed. Sabio quickly switched out mags and closed his eyes as she continued firing.

Desmond pushed his way through the heap of bodies. He got to his feet, a bloodied and beaten man. He assumed his fighting stance, ready for more, but there were no more. The shooting had stopped. The room had grown quiet. The black suits lay on the ground, motionless.

There was applause in the room. Desmond staggered around. Roberto Gonzalez was applauding from the comfort of his desk. Suddenly, the executive doors opened gracefully. High heels attached to a familiar shape clicked their way inside the room.

"So you're the one who kept interrupting my tour," Madeline said as she removed the blue scrunchie from her hair. With one shake of her head, her hair straightened out to the top of her shoulders.

"Oh crap," Desmond uttered under his breath.

"I never forget a face, but you kept yours hidden well."

It was true. Desmond had kept his face hidden behind the brochure every time he spoke. This was why no one had been able to spot him talking.

"This is going to be so exciting." Madeline giggled and cracked her neck and knuckles. "The things I'm going to do to you. I'm going to make you wish you never interrupted my tour."

Roberto cleared his throat.

"Oh, and I'm going to make you wish you never bothered Mr. Gonzalez. I hope you're ready for me, because I'm ready for you."

Madeline screamed and leapt into the air. Desmond stepped to the side and watched Madeline crash hard into Roberto's desk. She was knocked unconscious. The Superspy looked to Roberto for an explanation.

"She's not a fighter. Just a very dedicated employee." Roberto stood up and pulled out a switchblade.

Desmond got ready. Silver Fox took aim. There was no telling what this man was capable of. But oddly enough, Roberto opened his shirt and threw the blade at Desmond, who caught it instinctively.

"Go on! Take it! Take it!" Roberto lay flat against his desk. "The things I do for my beloved *compañia*. I would rather die than give chu my recipe. Take the heart!"

"I'm not taking your heart. Why do you keep saying that?"

"Because that's what chu must do to know what the secret ingredient is."

Desmond was confused.

"I had it surgically attached to *mi corazón* to protect its secret. You'll have to kill me if you want to know what it is."

Desmond sighed heavily. "Can't you just tell me what it is?"

"I can't. Only my beating heart can tell chu."

Desmond placed handcuffs on Roberto instead. He wasn't planning on cutting the man's chest open with a switchblade.

He escorted Roberto Gonzalez out of the black tower. They walked casually through the factory grounds with many of Roberto's men waking up with headaches from tranquilizer rounds. Agency helicopters surrounded the perimeter. Men rushed out to take possession of Roberto, his soldiers, and his factory.

"Get him to the vault," Desmond shouted over the roaring blades.

"Yes, sir."

"Hold up!" Sabio shouted over the noise. He approached Roberto Gonzalez, who looked at the pudgy agent with distaste. "Tell us where the mixing plant is."

"I don't know what chu are talking about."

"The Great Feast was a learning experience for you. After it happened, you knew better than to mix everything in the same location. If you won't tell us what the secret ingredient is, at least tell us where the raw batch is being mixed."

Roberto was quiet. Sabio pulled out a picture of Anthony and held it up to Roberto's face.

"Remember Humberto Diaz? This is his son. You ruined his life before it even had a chance to start. He will never have the opportunities that you took for granted growing up because of what happened to his father. Do the right thing. Seek forgiveness. Tell us where it is so this doesn't happen to someone else."

Silver Fox and Desmond watched anxiously to see if the man would say anything.

"Tell us," Sabio urged him.

Roberto half smiled and leaned close to Sabio. "Number thirteen," he finally said.

"Thank you." Sabio turned to the agents. "Get him out of here."

They nodded and strapped Roberto into his seat. The trio watched the helicopter lift off into the sky and roar its way toward the distant rising sun.

"You still need me?" Silver Fox asked, still looking at the horizon.

"No, but thank you for all your help—"

She was gone. A wisp in the wind. The dynamic duo turned to each other for an explanation, but neither could think of one.

Chapter 15

Pics

"Sir." An agent interrupted Stencil's midday mustache trimming. "Transmission coming in. It's from Billy Bob Billy Jeff Jenkins!"

"On screen," Stencil commanded. He stood up from his chair and watched the screen carefully, his left whiskers bushier than the ones on his right.

The message was without video or sound. It was a series of pictures showcasing Billy Bob's newly renovated and squeaky-clean secret lair. The last image showed a big red button with a fat finger hovering over it. The caption below the picture read, *Twelve hours left, Superspy!*

End of transmission.

Chapter 16

Warehouse Thirteen

Warehouse thirteen wasn't heavily fortified like its brother. Nor did it possess structural dominance that screamed the Gato Negro empire. The warehouse lay inside the unattractive manufacturing district of New Haven, a district typically known for hobos and shantytowns. One glance at the run-down facility, and no one could have guessed at the destructive potential lying in wait. The building was simple right down to its rectangular design, triangular tarnished metal roof, and the faded number thirteen across its green rustic metal facade. What it did showcase, however, was a slanting fence perimeter, out-of-shape security guards, and employees who dressed and resembled people from the disco era and not scientists.

Perhaps the look was a front, designed to ward off any suspicion. Perhaps Roberto Gonzalez owned every warehouse in the district and ran it like a stage show by paying actors to appear to look busy everywhere, including the passerby's, roach coaches, hobos and shantytowns. Whatever the case was, Roberto kept warehouse thirteen inconspicuous and out of sight from the rest of the world.

"No one make a move," Stencil spoke into every agent's ear. He was leading the assault from Central Command.

Field agents were itching for a fight. This was their moment—the all-or-nothing clash they had been waiting for. The adrenaline was so high you could smell the scent of men's underwear in the air. But Stencil needed his men to keep calm by maintaining a low profile. Now was not the time to do anything. Now was the time to be patient. This gave field agents very little choice but to wander the district aimlessly. Some lounged in front of taco trucks, while others sat at makeshift outdoor cafés, carefully monitoring the target from one block away. They were all in anticipation for the magic words to be whispered into their earpieces: *hocus pocus*. Then the games could begin.

"All of you move *only* when I say you move. Copy?"

"Copy," all one hundred agents responded simultaneously, producing a blowback of sound that translated into a deafening, high-pitched squawk.

If any of the security guards from warehouse thirteen had actually been doing their jobs and paying attention for any suspicious activity, they would have spotted every agent removing his ear piece and shaking off the blowback. Luckily for the Agency, the security guards were too busy taking naps.

Two blocks away, parked alongside the train tracks, was the silver cargo van. Desmond was having a hard time suiting up into his infiltration outfit. He was sore and bruised from the scuffle he'd endured six hours ago. Every movement he made hurt so much that it left Sabio with no choice but to help the Superspy into his outfit, like a parent would a child.

"Ouch…easy."

"Come on, man. Ain't that bad, is it?" Sabio strapped the tactical vest tightly around Desmond's torso, causing a painful grunt. "All done."

Desmond gave himself a quick once-over. He posed for Sabio. "What you think?"

"Not bad."

"Kind of makes my butt look big, don't you think?"

"I wouldn't know. I don't normally check out men's butts."

The two laughed like old friends—but in this case, as new friends. Since the Gato Negro mission, the duo had unknowingly lowered their guards and begun working as a team. Their long, awkward, silent road trips were now replaced by constant chitchat about the mission, but mostly about themselves. Sabio confessed to Desmond that blue was his favorite color, and that his favorite dish was pizza. In his spare time, he loved to read, write, and draw. He also explained how his parents were the reason why he got into computers.

"They would always fight," he told Desmond. "So, I would play Atari to tune them out. When I got older, Atari became computers. I was also into comic books. I wanted to be a superhero," he laughed. "The tech stuff came easy, and so I thought, what if I become the coolest superhero with high-tech gadgetry? I could help people…maybe even help kids who grew up like me," Sabio became quiet. He drove like such for minutes. "The Agency recruited me after college," he continued. "I was excited. I was actually going to become a secret agent, but none of that panned out. I passed the written test but failed the physical ones," he laughed nervously. "How did you end up with the Agency?"

"Darby," Desmond answered.

"Agent Darby?" Sabio responded with a hint of admiration.

"Yup,"

"That guy's a legend. How…how did he find you?"

"Foster care," he answered, and noted the curious look on Sabio's face. His brain was churning up more questions that he could possibly muster in one breath. "I'll tell you more about it next time," Desmond reassured Sabio's curious mind.

And that's how it went from then on out. The two agents continued talking about sports and hobbies. The companionship was welcomed even if neither wanted to admit that they were becoming friends.

"Think he'll show?" Sabio asked, looking at the distant warehouse.

"That's a good question." Desmond reclined against the cargo van, wincing in pain. "He's a pretty sharp guy."

"Yeah, but no way he'd miss this. I put *X* through all the channels. He knows it's here."

"In that case…there's a pretty good chance that he might show up."

"And when he does, we take him in on sight"—Sabio jumped onto the hood of the car—"put the cuffs on him, and ship his redneck ass back to Black Portal, where he belongs. And then…we go home." Sabio savored the sound of his last words. "Back to bed and afternoon pizza. Back to online gaming and drawing." He looked up into the afternoon sky and lost himself in the moment. "What about you?" he asked, not taking his eyes off the sky. "What are you looking forward to?"

The question caught Desmond by surprise. He hadn't given a single thought to anything but the mission. His mind had been obsessed with the capture of Billy Bob Billy Jeff Jenkins. As pleasing as the thought of sleep was, he heard his inner voice utter, *Aliana*. For the first time since the beginning of the mission, his thoughts raced back to their moment on the couch. Her laughter. Her smile. Her smell and her delicate touch. It all seemed like a lifetime ago, but it had only been four days. He wanted to see her again more than anything.

"That reminds me." Sabio jumped off the hood. He walked into the back of the van and came out carrying a stainless steel case. "I have goodies in case you're interested."

"I'm very interested."

Sabio set the case down on top of the hood and flicked both locks, carefully unveiling three devices snuggled into grooves of gray protective foam.

"XM-35 supergun." He pulled out the first device, handing it over to Desmond, who weighed the three-pound gun in both hands. "Can shoot explosive rounds and leave a good-size dent."

"How big?"

"Big enough to fit a midsize car."

"Damn." Desmond attached the gun to the back of his utility belt.

"Smoke pellets." Sabio carefully lifted out a two-pound bag full of what looked like gray marbles. "Each one is filled with enough smoke to cover three thousand square feet."

Desmond whistled and took the bag, securing it safely inside his front vest pocket.

"Now this here I like to call the X-nigma." Sabio held out a glossy-black prism device.

Desmond took it, unsure what to make of it. He held it against the sun but looked away from its refracting light. "What does it do?" Desmond attached it to the side of his belt.

"I don't know." Sabio snickered. "That's why it's called the X-nigma. Just pieced it together. It's got firepower, a few emergency countermeasures. I'm not sure what it does, but whatever that is, it's going to be spectacular." He waved his hands in the air like a magician after a trick.

The dynamic duo then rested quietly against the cargo van once more. Both were going to take advantage of the R and R before Stencil's call to action. Sabio busied himself with his phone; Desmond closed his eyes and enjoyed the cold breeze that came and went.

A screeching cry pried opened his eyes. The sky had caught on fire, turning bright yellow-red from several traversing colossal flames. Desmond watched closely as they exploded into several buildings. Several more emerged, followed by massive explosions. New Haven was on fire.

A powerful blast rocked the building behind them, collapsing the structure on top of the agents. Desmond pushed and crawled his way out from a mountain of concrete and rebar.

"Sabio." He coughed uncontrollably from the soot in the air. "Sabio," he called out again, searching the smoke-filled area for his partner, moving frantically through a cloud of ash debris that was once a set of buildings.

Desmond came to a dead stop once he found his partner. Sabio was buried under a mountain of concrete. Rebar had pierced his body. The man was dead.

"We're too late." Stencil's panic-stricken voice raced over Desmond's earpiece. "He's fired every rocket. The war has started."

Billy Bob Billy Jeff Jenkins had called their bluff and fired his rockets. He wasn't interested in the sauce after all. It was all a ruse to distract them.

Aliana.

Desmond paused.

Is she all right?

The Superspy stumbled through the streets like a man drunk. He searched for a way out of the fiery inferno; in his search, he caught sight of an army marching through fire. Leading the march was a tall, slender shape with green, glowing eyes. The shape spotted Desmond and raised its black hand into the air. The army stopped. It pointed at the Superspy. The army aimed their rifles. It closed its black hand into a tight fist. The army fired. The bullets tore through Desmond, cutting him down to pieces until there was nothing left except for a slab of meat on top of burning asphalt.

"Superspy! Superspy!"

Desmond woke up and found Sabio shaking him violently.

"Wake up!"

Desmond sat up quickly. It was a dream. There were no bombs, no burning buildings. The air around him lacked the smell of burning debris. The only change had come from day turning into night.

"He's here." Sabio pointed past the railroad tracks, down the alleyway, to warehouse thirteen, where four stealth planes were hovering over its metal roof, flooding the grounds with bright lights.

"No one make a move until the target is identified," Stencil commanded through his transmitter.

Warehouse security guards rushed out and opened fire at the stealth planes. They screamed in Spanish about aliens and anal probing. The stealth planes spooled their turret guns and returned fire, shredding the men in half. The remaining survivors dropped their guns and raced into the streets in a desperate sprint for their lives. The stealth planes fired rockets, causing the men to explode into slabs of flesh.

Soldiers clad in black gear rappelled from out of the sky, racing toward the warehouse doors. They planted explosives and quickly scattered away.

Boom!

The explosion rocked the foundation of the building, causing it to slant askew and catch on fire. The doors fell apart. Scientists staggered out, dazed and battered. Their chests burst open from gunfire by the elite team of soldiers. A heavily armed group of Roberto's men came charging out, firing from within the smoke, but were easily dispatched as well. The soldiers rushed into the burning warehouse. The sounds of gunfire did nothing to drown out the screams from the men and women hiding inside. The gunfire stopped. Soldiers raced back out from the thick smoke, carrying crates of the raw batch mixed with ingredient X.

"Has anyone spotted the target?" Stencil shouted, upset over the chaos.

Desmond quickly took to his binoculars. No Billy Bob in sight. Suddenly, a gunshot rang out from the rooftops across the warehouse. Then another, and then another.

The soldiers looked up, dropped the crates, took cover, and fired back.

"Who's firing?" Stencil screamed, which only seemed to encourage everyone to jump in.

By now, many of the agents were engaging the enemy. There was so much chaos and confusion over the radio that Desmond pulled out his earpiece and threw it away.

A stealth plane landed on the ground and provided cover for its soldiers. It then opened its forward hatch and released more soldiers into the mix. They provided cover while others picked up the crates and hurried them inside.

Desmond sprinted down the alleyway.

"Stay here," he yelled at his partner, knowing that Sabio was chasing after him.

He could hear Sabio's voice trailing off into the distance. "Wait."

Desmond raced across the street, feeling the aches and pains of his sore muscles. With one swift motion, he jumped over the warehouse fence and swiftly hid behind one of the cars in the parking lot. The soldiers were too preoccupied with the field agents across the street to notice him. From where Desmond hid, he could see the belly of the plane. It wasn't far. He only needed the right moment to race inside.

A stealth plane spun on its axis, turning its crosshairs into the agents firing from the building across the street. It unleashed a barrage of rockets that brought the structure down in seconds.

This was the moment Desmond had been waiting for. He hurried through the thick wall of dust and debris to reach the belly of the plane. Two clicks behind were the soldiers, also taking advantage of the moment to escape. They picked up the last remaining crate and rushed inside the plane. The hatch closed. Its blades spun to life, lifting the sleek V-shaped craft into the air. The remaining three planes unloaded the last of their payload into the warehouse district before blasting off, leaving the area in fiery limbo.

Sabio watched the planes disappear into the night sky. "Good luck," he said, knowing that Desmond had made his way inside. Hopefully he would see him again.

At roughly the same time, Roberto Gonzalez sat, and drank from a small cup of coffee with shaky hands. He was nervous— although he shouldn't be nervous. He was being held captive by the Agency at a top-secret location, locked up inside an impenetrable steel prison vault capable of withstanding several exploding rockets. There was nothing to worry about. That's what they'd told him. And that's what he kept telling himself despite the screams. It made no difference how thick the vault walls were; they did nothing to block out the screams and the sound of gunfire coming from the outside. The very ground trembled from an unseen force that rushed through Agency men like a charging bull. There was nothing to protect him from what was coming. Not even the thirty inches of thick steel that made up his cell.

The violent rumbling came to an abrupt stop before the vault. Roberto Gonzalez watched in terror as the vault door was bent and then crushed like a beer can and tossed aside. He stared unblinkingly at the gaping mouth of his cell, waiting for the nightmare to stomp its way inside. An Agency soldier flew inside instead. His body was thrown into the vault with such force that it stuck to the wall from splattered intestines.

It took its first step inside. The ceiling lights flickered from the weight of its heavy foot. It took its second step inside, followed by its colossal torso that bent its way through the vault opening. It used its muscular arms to leverage the rest of its thick frame inside as the back of its head forced itself against the ceiling, shattering the lights. It glared at Roberto with a pair of faded blue eyes.

Roberto could do nothing but tremble out of fear.

"I never agreed to any kind of bushering from chur king," Roberto said nervously.

The broad shadow stood unmoved.

"I thought chu people just wanted my sauce as an after-party celebration. I never agreed to reveal its true *potencial* to any of chu."

The shadow grunted. Roberto felt a rush of hot air blow through his body.

"I won't give chu my recipe. Chu can tell him that. If he wants it, then he will have to take it from my beating heart—"

Its massive fist plunged through Roberto Gonzalez's chest along with the chair he sat in. The giant lifted him into the air and examined the horrified expression on Roberto's face.

Roberto took in his last breaths of life before the massive hand shook him off like a fly on its wrist. Roberto's lifeless body plopped onto the ground. The giant opened its large palm and found a beating heart with a tiny plastic bag attached to it.

It plucked the tiny bag away with its thick fingertips and then tossed the beating heart onto the ground before stepping on it.

Chapter 17

Dangerous Games

They were in celebration mode, and rightly so. They had just scored a major victory over the Agency. To celebrate, they mocked, bragged, and laughed over their death counts. One solider fell to his knees and impersonated a man begging for his life, showing a picture of his wife and kids.

*"Please...please...*I have a *family."*

"What did you do?" a fellow soldier asked, grinning with excitement.

"I thought about it like he asked...and then put two holes into the picture that came out the back of his head." He laughed.

They all laughed. It was their sick and twisted form of combative group orgy after a battle. In their minds, those weren't innocent people from warehouse thirteen that they had just killed. No.

They were enemies of the Black Hand, and all enemies of the Black Hand were shown no mercy. That's how it was and how it would always be.

It took everything Desmond had not to break the compartment door open and do away with these men. No tranquilizer rounds this time, only full-metal slugs. From where he lay, he could easily dispatch six of them before they could figure out what was happening. He would take pleasure in watching their heads explode into brain matter, bringing a touch of color to an otherwise sterile interior. Or he could blow the interior wide open with his XM-35 supergun and grin at the sight of their bodies getting sucked out into the open sky, flailing to a horrific death.

Easy, Superspy, easy.

Desmond took a deep breath. The mission came first. He was in prime position, more than he had ever been in the past four days, to bring an end to it all. Patience was needed here. Not carelessness. Operation Hidden Vault came to mind. No, he couldn't afford to be careless this time.

"OK, ladies, we're about to make our descent," the intercom chimed.

The soldiers returned to their seats and buckled up, still grinning in the wake of their celebration. The interior shook aggressively from the descent. It dropped, feeling like an elevator ride but on steroids, spiraling down to the bottom floor from the one hundredth. Desmond felt his stomach rise to midchest level. He became dizzy and was on the verge of throwing up. The soldiers were having the opposite reaction. They cheered and raised their hands in the air as one would on a roller-coaster ride. When the plane eased into its normal level of descent, Desmond felt his stomach crawl back to his abdomen. The plane swayed a dizzying left and then a dizzy right. It paused in midair for a brief moment before settling down with a loud *thud* to mark the end of its journey.

"Touchdown," the intercom announced. The soldiers clapped.

Seat belts were unbuckled, and boots made their way to the crates, picking them up one after the other. Once the forward hatch came undone, the soldiers marched their way down the ramp, continuing to celebrate their victory and new collective booty.

Desmond kicked the compartment door open once he was convinced that he was the only one left inside. He crawled from underneath the seats, stood up and made his way toward the forward hatch. They weren't far behind. He could still make out the soldiers' laughter. When he stepped foot onto the ramp, he saw it and stopped. It was all so eerily beautiful.

The outside air sparkled from miniature floating stars. They buzzed around him playfully and stuck to him from head to toe. Desmond reached out and watched one float gingerly into the palm of his hand. When he looked closer, he realized that it wasn't a star at all but a tiny speck of sand.

The glittering sand that cascaded from the edge of the circular opening resembled an endless waterfall accompanied by the moon and stars. It was a beautiful spectacle to behold—a spectacle that came to an abrupt end from the sound of mechanical locks coming undone. Gears followed next. The circular opening gradually converged onto itself like the iris of a camera. Once sealed, the area below was faintly bathed in red by lights that hung crookedly in midair. They revealed bits and pieces of a massive hangar.

Everywhere Desmond turned, he could make out stealth planes. They were in the hundreds, parked in formation for the next assault. The Agency had underestimated Billy Bob Billy Jeff Jenkins. He had the arsenal to strike anywhere, and hard. If the hangar were only a small fraction of the mad scientist's strength, Desmond could only imagine how large the rest of the facility was, including the military personnel.

Desmond moved swiftly across the hangar floor, staying in the shadows and out of sight from patrolling guards. He raced toward the area where he'd last heard the soldiers' laughter and knew he was close when he came within a few short yards of a glowing light source.

Desmond stopped and backed against the rock wall. He peeked into the light and was greeted by his own reflection. He moved in, a foot at a time, his gun lowered by his side. The passageway was narrow, white, and brightly lit. The walls and floor were made of a glossy material that mirrored his every move. When he reached the end of the passageway, he turned the corner cautiously, only to see the same stretch of glossy whiteness waiting for him. Desmond experienced déjà vu three more times before it left him feeling disorientated and vulnerable. When he backtrailed, he came to a dead end that was not there a moment ago. It invited him to go through a different passageway instead. Suddenly, more dead ends and more passageways that forced him left and right. And right and left. The white maze seemed to be enjoying its time with him. A dark rectangular opening from farther down caught his attention. No doubt it had been put there for Desmond's purpose.

The Superspy approached the opening cautiously, convinced that someone was watching him from inside. A spark of light came from the center of the room. The source was a monitor resting above a pedestal. The screen fizzled when he came within two steps. A title materialized when he came within one: *The Second Great Feast.*

Segments from an animated short played out, depicting rockets fueled with Agua Dulce BBQ sauce. Stealth planes were then shown hovering over continents, launching a full-scale assault. Their missiles struck buildings, landmarks, and heavily populated areas. Lands were left in flames. Bloodied survivors walked the devastation, notably drenched in BBQ sauce from the explosions. They fought each other till they began to feast on their adversaries' flesh. The image pulled back from the carnage to a full view of Earth with a red stain eating away at the blue oceans and green lands. All that remained was a red, bloodied orb. The segment ended with images of barren wastelands and collapsed cities. An army then marched the lands, waving banners with the insignia of the Black Hand.

The computer screen shut off. The lights in the corridor followed suit. Desmond was left in darkness. He switched on the tactical light mounted on the tip of his gun and turned around carefully before making his way back into the white, glossy maze.

"You didn't really think that it would be that easy. Did you, Superspy?"

Desmond stopped. He recognized the redneck voice.

"That was a clever plan, letting me know about them untouched batches, but it also brought you out in the open, didn't it? And here you thought you had the upper hand."

Billy Bob Billy Jeff Jenkins laughed. His laughter vibrated off the walls, encompassing Desmond in a cage of mockery, making him unaware of where the laughter was coming from.

"How fast can you run, Superspy?"

A white door slid over the rectangular opening behind Desmond. Shortly after, several dozen spikes rose from within the white walls as they began to close in on each other.

"I guess we're about to find out," Billy Bob snickered.

Desmond raced down the corridor, his tactical light bouncing sideways. Rows of spikes grew from one row to the next. The walls moved quickly now, giving him mere seconds to escape the passageway. As he reached the corner, he turned in time to witness the corridor crush itself to bits and pieces—spikes, walls, and all.

"Not bad, Superspy. Not bad. Do it again, a few *hundred* times."

Desmond spun back around. More spikes, with faster-moving walls. He dashed through the danger once more, successfully making it across in the nick of time, only to find another passageway with faster-growing spikes and even faster-moving walls. He raced down the corridor a third time, this time feeling the pain from his overspent body.

Boom!

Success but only by a fraction of a second. Another corridor gone, with a new one starting up. Desmond lost count after the tenth corridor. He was beyond tired. His muscles were at the point of overexhaustion. His legs were turning into mush. It didn't matter how many passageways he beat—more sprang into action. There was no end in sight to Billy Bob's white maze of horror. But the Superspy dug deep and sprinted like he'd never sprinted before, nicking his left shoulder and calf on his last run before crashing on the ground with everything behind him shattering to pieces.

Desmond pushed himself off the floor and limped into the next stretch that was already halfway from imploding. At the far end of the corridor was a circular opening with the word *Exit* blinking above it profusely.

"Think you can make it?" Billy Bob taunted.

Hurt, tired, and drained, Desmond hopped his way toward the exit. There was still a long way to go when the exit disappeared behind another sliding door. This triggered the walls and spikes to move at a greater pace.

Desmond pulled out his XM-35 supergun, aimed, and fired. The explosive round blew apart the far end, leaving a gaping hole. He sped up, gnashing his teeth from the unbearable pain coursing through his body. Just as the spikes were about to impale flesh and bone, the secret agent somersaulted through the opening, landing face down onto concrete.

Boom!

Desmond was breathing heavily. He was gassed.

"I'm impressed. Takes a lot to impress me."

Desmond forced himself to his feet, dripping in sweat. He now found himself inside a semidark rectangular room.

"Can you dodge bullets, Superspy?"

Turret guns dropped from the four corners of the ceiling. Four more rose off the floor. Desmond felt the heat from their lasers tagging his arms, legs, chest, and head. One laser was particularly fond of a spot between his eyes. They spooled up. Desmond reached into his vest and swung his right arm into the room. Thick smoke quickly covered the area. The turrets let loose, swiveling blindly at the thick haze, releasing every punishing round ruthlessly till their nozzles overheated and melted from the burst of fire. Thick smoke clung to the air for a prolonged period of time. When it dissipated, it showed the room full of bullet holes the size of beach balls.

Desmond stood triumphantly tall in the middle of it all, fully intact.

The wall directly across parted sideways, unveiling a third semidark, empty space. Curiosity invited Desmond inside. He was hesitant at first, but with nowhere else to go, he proceeded inside. The walls behind him closed shut.

The third room was emitting a hissing noise from the ceiling. A layer of steam hung across the room, causing the Superspy to sweat instantaneously.

"I bet you taste real good with BBQ sauce."

"You're a sick, sick man."

"Am I? I'm not sick. I think they're the ones who are sick."

From out of the shadows staggered a dozen soldiers.

Desmond took to his fighting stance, though it was poor, tired, and riddled with aches and pain. But the soldiers were acting strange. They weren't reaching for their guns. They were reaching for him instead, snarling with red, beaming eyes.

"I gave them a touch of the good stuff, if you know what I mean. But I think they're still hungry."

The soldiers pounced on Desmond immediately. The Superspy pulled out his gun and opened fire, hitting several of his marks in the head. More shapes staggered out from the shadows, amassing into a horde of hands and snarling mouths. They went for his arms, legs, and face, fighting each other for a chance at raw flesh.

Desmond dropped his gun in the struggle. The infected soldiers pinned him to the floor, their mouths salivating from hunger. Desmond kicked every mouth and punched every face that came inches from his own.

In the midst of his struggles, ceiling panels came undone section by section. Columns of fire roared out, burning the soldiers into crispy shapes.

Before hungry mouths could take a chunk off Desmond, the remaining panels gave away, leaving the Superspy to stare directly into a gaping black hole. It hissed to life, discharging a stream of gas before it caught on fire.

The column of fire immersed the masses into the fiery hell that had taken the third room…Superspy and all.

Chapter 18

Billy Bob Billy Jeff Jenkins

Four soldiers came bursting through the doors, wheeling a gurney of burnt flesh.

They set and locked the gurney in place and then took two steps back to stand at attention, allowing Billy Bob Billy Jeff Jenkins to have a closer inspection of his creation.

Billy Bob circled the gurney, admiring his handiwork of burnt zombie-soldier corpses encasing the Superspy. The charcoal statue captured the final moments of his life: his arms shielding his face from the oncoming flames that burned him to a crisp.

"That's what I'm talking about!" Billy Bob clapped excitedly. "I like my Superspies well done." He tied a bib around his neck and produced a knife and fork from his pockets. "Who's hungry?"

The charred mass shook, catching everyone by surprise. A fist broke through the brittle surface, dropping a prism device on the floor. Another hand broke free, using the gurney as leverage to pull its remaining self out. The charred mess then burst apart in a swirling wake of black confetti.

Billy Bob was speechless at first when wrinkles began forming across his face. Facial muscles stretched backward into a full-on excited grin as the man applauded, excited to see the Superspy while everyone else in the room remained in a state of shock.

Desmond jumped off the gurney and dusted himself off.

"Now, that's what I'm talking about! That's an entrance! Yeah." He continued clapping, looking at his guards, who knew it was in their best interest to join him.

Desmond sized up the situation. He was inside the control room surrounded by monitors, sparkling lights, mainframe computers, and twenty clapping soldiers. Under his current status, he should have been worried, but the X-nigma had given him some of his strength back. He felt good.

"Impressive, Superspy, pretty impressive. You survived my spikes of doom." Billy Bob walked around the secret agent, admiring his tenacity. "And you survived my turrets of doom. And you also survived...my flames of doom," Billy Bob stopped, meeting the Superspy eye to eye. "Impressive...but not as impressive as my newly cleaned secret lair." His voice boomed with thrilling excitement, like that of a game show host. "What do you think?"

Desmond examined the room. It was clean. In fact, he had just realized how clean everything had been since he'd arrived. The stealth planes were clean, the hangar was spotless, and even the white maze of horror was unblemished.

Desmond nodded. "Not bad."

"Not bad? *Not bad?* It's clean, dammit!" Billy Bob screamed. "It took me days to get it this clean. You tell me who else has a secret lair this clean. *No one!* That's who. You can't conquer the world in filth. You can leave it in filth, but you can't conquer it in filth. That's why the best bad guys are the ones who clean as a profession. The whole point of conquering the world is to clean it up."

An alarm came on. It startled everyone in the room except for Billy Bob. It seemed to amuse him.

"Looks like your time is up." Billy Bob glanced up at the counter above everyone's head. It blinked zero repeatedly.

"Time to unleash the zombie apocalypse on the world and bear witness to the second Great Feast. Then soon, very soon, the Black Hand will rise from the ashes of the former world and lead us into prosperity in a new world order."

"Not without ingredient X," Desmond added.

This shut up Billy Bob.

"You don't have it. And you need it."

"That's where you're wrong, Superspy. *Wrong! Wrong! Wrong!*" Billy Bob stomped his foot like an angry child. "I got ingredient X! Thanks to you and your Agency's mediocre plan to lure me to warehouse thirteen. You gave me a sample of the raw batch. It only takes a few drops to cause the sickness. There's more than

enough for a first strike. And special thanks to my friend over there…"
Billy Bob motioned behind him.

Desmond looked past the ranting lunatic and gained a small
glimpse of two shadowy figures watching the scene from a safe
distance before Billy Bob blocked his view with a small plastic bag.

"I have the origins of ingredient X," he concluded.

Desmond stared at the small plastic bag, unsure what he was
looking at.

"Seeds." Billy Bob shook the bag. "Tiny, dancing seeds."

The mad scientist laughed when he noticed the sad revelation
taking shape over the Superspy's face.

"That's right," he said, "Roberto Gonzalez is dead. And in his
death, he gave us *chile sangre*." He shook the tiny bag again. "The rare
chili plant from South America that caused the extinction of the
Mayan empire. Historians and anthropologists will lead you to believe
that their extinction was owed to clan warfare. Wrong! They ate
themselves to death. That's why they went extinct. They couldn't

resist the scrumdiddlyumptious taste of human flesh. We've already began to plant these little babies into my nursery, and once they are full grown, we will strike a second blow to the world. Then soon, very soon, the world will eat itself to death, and the Black Hand will rise from the ashes of the former world—"

"You said that already."

"Dawning a new age of prosperity and new world order—"

"You said that already."

"I'm saying it again for emphasis, dammit! You're just mad because you won't be able to do anything to stop it."

"Try me."

This amused Billy Bob, who folded his arms, about to laugh. "And how do you plan to stop me when I have everyone pointing a gun at you? Including the maid."

Everyone in the room had a gun pointed at Desmond, including the maid, who was a short Mexican woman with a set of serious eyes.

Desmond lowered his hand to his holster. A tense moment befell the room. Sweat trickled down faces. Eyes darted back and forth. Hearts skipped beats. Bodies shook nervously. Everyone was waiting for the first move.

The moment was abruptly broken by the ringing of someone's cell phone. No one moved. The phone kept ringing and ringing.

"Anyone gonna answer that?" Billy Bob asked, frustrated.

Everyone in the room reached into their pockets and pulled out their cell phones. A mixture of *hello*s was heard, followed by *it's not me*. The phone was still ringing.

"Whose phone is that?" Billy Bob was now visibly upset.

Desmond felt the vibration coming from his pant leg. "Hold on. It's me."

The group was annoyed. Desmond pulled out his phone as he kept everyone in suspense. "Hello?"

"*Where are you?*"

Desmond's eyes widened. He was sure everyone else had heard her voice.

"Aliana?" he whispered.

"Yes, *Aliana*!" she screamed. "Where are you?"

"Uh…" Desmond turned to everyone, who looked the other way, not wanting to get involved. "Work," he said reluctantly, cringing at his response.

"Work? You're at work? Are you serious?"

Desmond pulled the phone as far away from his ear as he could; her voice was gnawing away at his eardrums.

"This was supposed to be our weekend getaway, and you're off playing at work while I'm stuck up here all by myself. And how the hell is it Thursday when yesterday was Saturday?"

Desmond said nothing. He was a bit embarrassed.

"Hello?"

"Yes."

"Yes, what? Is that all you've got to say?"

"Uh—"

"You know what? Fine. Don't say anything. Stay at work. I don't care anymore."

"Wait. Baby—"

Click!

Desmond stared at the phone in disbelief. Aliana had never hung up on him before. Not in the two years they had been together.

"Damn." Billy Bob chuckled. "I could hear that all the way over here. Everyone else hear that?"

The room murmured and nodded.

"I don't know what's worse, killing you or letting you go back home to that. But then again…it doesn't matter anymore, does it?" he asked, slow and serious. "Not after I destroy the world." He grinned.

Without any more delay, Desmond whipped his pistol from his holster and opened fire in quick succession. The shots blew the guns away from Billy Bob's men, including the maid, who immediately massaged her wrist from the pain.

Desmond aimed his gun carefully at Billy Bob's head.

"What are you doing?" Billy Bob asked nervously.

"I'm gonna shoot you."

"Aren't you going to take me in?"

"No."

"Why not?"

"Because there's no point. You'll escape again, and your little game restarts."

"Well, yeah, that's how it always plays out."

"Not anymore. I had a perfect weekend planned with my girl, but you had to escape to conquer the world. I'm done. Best way to get rid of a problem is to get rid of it permanently."

"Wait! Won't you get in trouble with the Agency?"

"Wouldn't be the first time," Desmond said, about to pull the trigger.

"Wait! Wait! I'm sorry, Superspy. I'm sorry. I didn't realize you had it so rough. We're all sorry, right, fellas?"

Everyone nodded.

"See, we're all sympathetic to your cause," he said with a nervous grin.

"Tell it to my gun."

Desmond aimed. Billy Bob winced from the oncoming blast.

Boom!

The building rocked. Ceiling lights came undone and shattered on the floor.

Boom!

Everyone was pushed off balance. Sparks flew from the control room, creating a small fire.

Billy Bob tossed the maid over to Desmond, who caught her instantaneously, and raced out the exit.

The maid smiled nervously at the Superspy. "*Hola*," she said.

"*Hola*," he said in return and threw the maid into the arms of nearby soldiers, who stumbled backward on the floor.

The Superspy raced into a second white maze, anticipating moving walls and emerging spikes. But none showed themselves this time. Instead, lights blinked on and off from the nonstop pounding of distant explosions. From up ahead, he could make out Billy Bob's voice shouting to his men: "He's coming. Shoot. Shoot."

Desmond turned the corner and was met with three soldiers who were in the middle of taking aim. He reached behind him, pulled out his XM-35 supergun, and fired. Bodies were blown through the walls. He reloaded and turned the corner.

He could hear the redneck scientist scream, "Move! Move!"

Desmond turned to his right this time and went down a different passageway with soldiers opening fire. He pulled the trigger and watched their bodies blow apart. He reloaded. One last round.

"Get him, dammit! He won't stop."

Billy Bob raced up the corridor with six of his men racing in the opposite direction. They screeched to a stop, aimed, and shot at the oncoming Superspy, missing him from careless aim. Desmond fired and blew the men apart into strands of meat. He turned the next corner and saw a limping Billy Bob Billy Jeff Jenkins. He was out of breath, holding his right side. Desmond was only a short sprint-tackle away when twenty of Billy's men came charging to his rescue from around the turn. Five soldiers surrounded Billy Bob and escorted him down the passageway; the remaining fifteen stopped, knelt down on the floor, and took aim.

If Desmond was going to die, then they were going to have to unload every clip they had on him because he wasn't going to stop. He sped up. Rounds burst into the air. The soldiers toppled over one by one. Armed Agency men turned the corner and watched Desmond racing toward them. They lowered their guns.

"It's the Superspy," the team captain called out.

"Gun. Gun. Give me your gun," Desmond screamed, not stopping.

The team captain tossed his pistol at the running agent, who caught it and disappeared around the corner.

The white corridor was now filled with Agency soldiers in a deadly firefight with Billy Bob's men. Desmond flew through the dizzying passages, relying on the same instincts and newfound energy he'd had at Willow Brook. Thirty seconds later he was in the hangar, where an even greater battle was being fought. Explosions and rattling machine-gun fire filled the air. Desmond had no interest in joining this fight. He was after only one thing. He stopped and looked.

There, in the distance, he saw Billy Bob. His men were escorting him into the belly of a stealth plane.

As the hatch came undone, Billy Bob moved into the plane. He stopped short of the entrance, turned, and searched the battlefield. When his eyes met Desmond's, he smiled and waved. "Until next time, Superspy." He laughed.

The hatch closed. The plane powered on. The hangar floor rumbled from mechanical locks coming unhitched. The iris above opened slowly, introducing cascading sand into the battlefield, obscuring all visibility. The stealth plane launched into the air, fanning the sand, creating a dust storm.

Desmond pulled the trigger, but the bullets bounced off the plane's exterior like pebbles. The gun was not powerful enough to penetrate the hull of the plane. The Superspy watched helplessly as the stealth plane rose higher and higher.

Like a white flash of lightning, a bullet grazed the sky, taking out one of the twin-blade engines. The stealth plane leaned on its side, spiraling out of control. Another loud bang raced through the air, taking out the remaining spinning engine, sending the craft into a spiraling crash. The stealth plane exploded onto other aircraft, creating a destructive chain reaction of exploding metal.

Billy Bob coughed and crawled through shattered glass from the cockpit window. He staggered back to his feet, dazed and confused by the surrounding flames. From out of nowhere, he was tackled to the floor, turned over, and handcuffed.

"You're under arrest," Sabio said, out of breath.

Desmond emerged through the smoke, surprised to find his partner standing over Billy Bob, posing like a superhero; his arms to his side, his right leg resting on the mad scientist's back.

"I always wanted to say that." He smiled at Desmond.

Desmond smiled in return and nodded at his partner's handiwork. He looked up to the surrounding rafters and nodded to Silver Fox for bringing down the aircraft.

When the smoke finally cleared and the shooting had stopped, the Agency emerged victorious. Billy Bob's men had given up once they saw their leader captured. They were handcuffed into rows of chains, awaiting flying transport to Black Portal prison.

Desmond and Sabio forced Billy Bob Billy Jeff Jenkins to stand and watch his men and base come under Agency control.

"How did you find me?"

"The X-nigma. It released a surge of energy when you turned it on. It could be seen from space."

Desmond chuckled. "Of course it did."

"Wasn't hard after that."

They laughed; just like back at the cargo van, they laughed like two friends. This sickened Billy Bob. "You two should get a room."

"Don't be jealous because you have no friends, Billy Bob," Sabio responded.

That's when they all heard it. The unmistakable sound of screeching wheels. This caught everyone's attention: guards and prisoners alike. Everyone turned and spotted an old woman, wearing thick glasses, sporting a gray skirt and black blouse, wheeling an old man into the center of the hangar. She knelt down and whispered into the old man's ear and handed him a syringe before walking away.

"Oh, I got friends. Friends in dark places," Billy Bob said with a noticeable grin.

The old man raised the syringe high in the air and impaled it into his chest. His body went into convulsions. He fell onto the ground. Foam spewed from his mouth. His eyes rolled to the back of his head. He screamed in agony and crawled his way toward the agents. His chest and back expanded to incredible size and depth, shredding his clothes like second skin. His arms bulged with muscles, his skin rejuvenated, and his legs became as thick as tree trunks. He went from crawling to standing, just like the evolutionary man...only he stood two stories tall, a towering, muscular behemoth who stared at everyone with lifeless blue eyes.

"Hope you're ready for this, Superspy. Because it ain't over." The redneck scientist laughed.

Desmond's hands shook. That same feeling he'd experienced at the Devil's Balls came over him. That feeling was fear. Here was the brute force that had chased them that day. Desmond had avoided a confrontation with it then because he knew he wasn't ready for it, but he could do nothing to avoid it now.

With a thick, booming voice, the towering behemoth uttered something in Russian.

"What did he say?" Sabio asked.

"Long live the Black Hand," Desmond answered.

Chapter 19

The Showdown

Alexey Dorkhovich was born prior to World War I but fought in War World II. He was a Russian major with many under his command who knew him under a different name. The men called him, "Bomber" because he liked to make everything go *ka-boom*. He liked *ka-boom*. It was his favorite word: *ka-boom*. In fact, he was known to have a rocket launcher strapped to his back, with a leather sash of rockets wrapped diagonally across his muscular torso, always looking for an excuse to use them, which was all the time.

But *ka-boom* wasn't the only thing Dorkhovich was known for. He was also a physical specimen who enjoyed attention. The Nazis had reported on several occasions engaging a Russian infantry man sporting an unbuttoned shirt with torn sleeves and ripped pant-shorts who enjoyed flexing his muscular chest in the heat of battle and kissing his biceps after every fiery explosion that came from his rocket launcher. He was cruel to his victims, laughing hysterically at their flailing corpses, right before flexing his quadriceps and calves.

His blue eyes, blond hair, strong chin, and simple-minded words gave Dorkhovich the appearance of a mindless brute. But it was all a ruse. Dorkhovich was both muscular and intelligent. He organized and took part in the invasion of Nazi Germany with his deadly use of *ka-booms* that tore through the Nazi regime. During the Cold War, he formed part of the Soviet spy network by posing as a muscular auto mechanic with a thick, heavy Russian accent in the United States. He gained intelligence about the American lifestyle for the Soviet Union until it all came to a crashing end on June 13, 1990, with the official collapse of the Berlin Wall that marked the end of his days as a Soviet spy.

Dorkhovich cried like a little buff baby. He remained in the United States and continued to work as a mechanic, too ashamed to return back home. He felt partially responsible for the loss of the Cold War and spiraled into a deep depression over the years, wanting to end it all with a shotgun blast to the mouth.

Then came *the call.*

It came to a select few. It spoke about a new world order—about the Black Hand, which would rise from the ashes of the past and restore balance to the world. Western civilization would cease, along with world religions. The world would be organized into one common ideology, much like the Soviet Union had been in the past—only better.

All Dorkhovich had to do was wait till the appointed time. It would be worth it, he was told. No fame, money, or women could match the gifts waiting for him in the distant future. So Dorkhovich waited. He disappeared into obscurity in case the Americans decided to investigate him, and he never stayed in one place at a time. The Black Hand's underground network created a trust fund in his name to recompense the time. They had also assigned an attractive Russian woman to fulfill his every need and desire. The Sunny Side Retirement Home proved to be the perfect cover once old age set in. By then, no one would suspect that a sixty-two-year-old posed a threat to national security.

Dorkhovich never lost hope in the Black Hand. Even so close to death at ninety-two, he knew the time was near. He felt it through Elena's readings, and vowed to remain silent until the *time* came.

"It's time," the mysterious voice proclaimed over the phone. "The Black Hand has called upon you to return to action and help bring the new world order."

Dorkhovich was pleased. He was sneaked out of Sunny Side by Elena and administered the green elixir given to all secret agents of the Black Hand. It reinvigorated him with youth. It gave him unmatched power and towering heights. He felt unstoppable, like a bomb. *Ka-boom!*

Dorkhovich was ordered to assist the redneck scientist with whatever he needed as long as it did not stray from preparing the world for the new world order. Most importantly, he was ordered to do away with the Agency's top agent, the Superspy, as a show of strength from the Black Hand. The Superspy had narrowly escaped his demise at the Devil's Balls. But now, with so many watching, Dorkhovich was going to make him pay by tearing the super agent's body into a bloody goo of intestines.

Billy Bob Billy Jeff Jenkins could no longer contain himself. This was it. The final showdown. It's what the Black Hand had wanted all along. He laughed hysterically.

"Get him out of here." Desmond gave the order, keeping his eyes focused on the towering behemoth casually making its way toward him.

The transformation had left Dorkhovich in his early twenties, sporting a buzzed haircut. He was naked at first, when from out of nowhere came a large red flag possessing the Black Hand insignia. He tied it around his waist to use as a loincloth and smiled at everyone, right before flexing his muscles. The attention made Dorkhovich feel alive.

"It's time for a diaper change, Superspy, cuz I can smell the one you have on, and it reeks." Billy Bob laughed.

"That was just lame," Sabio replied.

"Get him the hell out of here!" Desmond gave the order a second time, but his men could not look away from the towering brute.

Finally, two Agency soldiers snapped out of their trance, and dragged Billy Bob away, who protested that he wanted to stay and see the fight. He was carried onto a waiting transport and airlifted out of the secret base.

Dorkhovich didn't care. His eyes were on the Superspy. He wasn't too concerned about Billy Bob. The scientist had failed, but the Black Hand would deal with him soon enough.

"Fire!" someone screamed.

The soldiers unleashed everything they had at the muscular specimen. The Russian behemoth laughed. Bullets bounced off him like pellets. He placed both hands against his hips, and flexed his pecs repeatedly like Ping-Pong paddles, swatting the bullets away, striking the men in the crossfire. When the agents ran out of ammo and frantically switched clips, the giant shouted something in Russian.

"What did he say?" Sabio asked nervously.

"He said that tickled," Desmond responded.

He spoke again. The men turned to Desmond for translation. "My turn."

Dorkhovich plucked a stealth wing off the ground with such ease that it horrified everyone immediately. He crumpled it inside his gigantic palms into a ball of jagged metal, took three steps forward, and bowled the metal ball with such speed and ferocity that it scooped many agents off the floor, pinning them splat against the cavern wall. Agency men unleashed another wave of bullets, which seemed to anger the behemoth this time. He scooped up more metal off the ground and hurled it at the men, creating a windstorm of metal shards. Everyone took cover. Some weren't so lucky and were cut in half by flying debris. Others were struck and sent flying across the hangar into dark obscurity to be impaled against the cavern wall like a piece of home décor.

Dorkhovich unleashed a war cry and charged at Desmond and his men. The floor shook with brute kinetic force. The raging bull ploughed into a group of soldiers, whose girly screams let out their last breaths. Dorkhovich backslapped several men, sending them twenty feet into the air to strike fiercely against the cavernous ceiling. The giant snatched one soldier and broke him in half. He tore another in half with his teeth and plucked the limbs off one soldier like one would to rose petals. He tore into stealth planes and pulled out missiles to use as grenades. He tossed them at the soldiers and laughed at the bodies exploding into bits.

"Ka-boom," he said, and kissed his biceps.

He then went into a frenzied state of mind, chasing, and stomping on everyone like insects, including Billy Bob's men. It didn't matter who he was killing. He just wanted to make everyone go splat. Billy Bob's men tried to run away, but the mass confusion of rattling chains caused them to run into each other. Dorkhovich grabbed hold of the restraints and swung them around and around in the air like a lasso. The men could be heard screaming, until the giant slammed the chains on the ground, killing them instantly. His focus was now on the Superspy, who stood a few feet away.

Dorkhovich was ready to charge when Desmond released the last of his gas pebbles. The giant immediately sucked the smoke into its mouth, and belched it out to the side, leaving the Superspy exposed.

Sabio pointed his trembling gun at the giant.

Dorkhovich noticed the pudgy man and smirked.

"No! Get out of here." Desmond pushed Sabio out of the way and was backslapped thirty feet into the air. His body struck the floor hard, bouncing a few feet more after the initial impact. Desmond picked himself up, his body swaying left and right, his face bloodied from the impact. He saw a blurry triangular shape rapidly advancing. He jumped out of the way, narrowly missing contact with the wing from an aircraft. Desmond stood back up, still in a state of haze, when he saw something else rushing toward him. It was Dorkhovich, only this time he wasn't quick enough to move out of the way.

Dorkhovich unleashed a powerful blow at the Superspy's tiny frame. But at the same time the air crackled with the sound of thunder. Dorkhovich was hit square in the chest and pushed back a few feet. His fist struck the ground instead, creating a deep crater.

Dorkhovich clenched his chest. He was angry. Another sound of thunder. The giant's head snapped back, pushing him off balance to fall butt first onto the floor. He screamed. He had just been humiliated by someone. The giant jumped to his feet. The ground shook with such force that it caused everything on the hangar floor to bounce two feet into the air. With his vision, he scanned the high ceiling, where he spotted a woman aiming a rifle at him.

Dorkhovich picked whatever metal scraps he could rummage off the floor and swung them at the woman. He even dug his nails into the concrete floor and hurled slabs of cement. He then charged and slammed his muscular shape into the side of the hangar she was hiding in. The ceiling wall collapsed, along with the rafters. Dorkhovich pulled himself out of the debris and rummaged through rock and metal until he found the woman, unconscious. He smiled and raised his foot into the air, ready to squash the petite female like a worthless cockroach.

"Hey!"

Dorkhovich paused, his foot in midair. He turned around and saw Desmond aiming his gun at him.

"I'm over here, stupid."

Dorkhovich grinded his teeth. He slammed his foot back onto the ground, narrowly missing Silver Fox by a few feet, and stomped his way toward the Superspy.

"The Black Hand will bring an end to your beloved country and its fake ideals. He will do away with your kings and queens and your false sense of democracy. The strong will reign over the weak."

"Whatever you say, *tiny*."

"*Tiny?*" Dorkhovich roared.

He leapt into a roaring charge. Desmond took aim and fired a slug into the giant's right eye, blinding him, slowing his charge. He fired again, into the giant's left eye this time. Dorkhovich covered his face with both hands, squinting in pain. Desmond fired at the giant's genitals next. This brought Dorkhovich to a complete stop, a foot short of the secret agent. Desmond took aim at the giant's toes in an attempt to bring him tumbling down, but failed to see the swooping left hand that snatched him off the ground. Desmond immediately felt the pressure from the squeezing hand. His bones cracked as the life inside of him was squeezed out of his lungs. With his free hand, Dorkhovich plowed deep into the belly of a destroyed stealth plane and pulled out another missile. He tore the cap off with his teeth and spat it on the floor. The bomb began to tick. He held it and Desmond close to his chest.

From across the hangar bay, Sabio was helping Silver Fox to her feet. The two watched Desmond try to pull the giant's hand apart, but the grip was too strong. The giant squeezed his every attempt, causing Desmond to scream in agony. The bomb's ticking was steadily increasing.

"As much as I wish to partake in the world to come, there must be sacrifices," Dorkhovich proclaimed out loud, his voice resonating off the destroyed hangar walls. "You and I will be the sacrifice the world needs to set everything in order. All hail the Black Hand!"

In that moment, the world had gone silent for Desmond. He closed his eyes and saw Aliana. Images of times spent together rushed through his mind. He had to see her again. He wasn't going to die like this. Not like this.

The Superspy inside came alive. He felt his body surge with a newfound strength. He pried open the giant's grip, which caught Dorkhovich by surprise. He squeezed even tighter. Desmond fought back, finally breaking free of the giant's hold, landing quickly on the ground. He pulled his right arm back and then swung deep into the giant's stomach with such strength that it knocked the air from out of his lungs, sending Dorkhovich a few feet back. Desmond leapt into the air and with a spinning back kick knocked a tooth from Dorkhovich's mouth, sending the giant back a few feet more. Dorkhovich screamed, but before he could do anything, the Superspy took hold of his left muscular arm and tossed him over his shoulder.

Boom!

Dorkhovich sat up. He was dazed, his mouth wide open with saliva pouring out when the missile was stuffed inside. Desmond hooked his left arm under the giant's strong jaw, interlocking his fingers with his right arm wrapped around the giant's square head. Dorkhovich reached up and desperately tried to pull the Superspy off. When that didn't work, he tried with both hands to break the tiny man in half like a pencil. Desmond wasn't going to let go. Dorkhovich had to be stopped. This was the only way.

The missile was ticking faster and faster.

"Desmond!" he heard Sabio scream.

"Get back!" he shouted.

Funny, Desmond thought. That was the first time Sabio had called him by his name. Up until then, it had always been *Super* or *Superspy*. He laughed. It looked like they were becoming friends after all.

The explosion blew Dorkhovich apart. Chunks of fiery meat, and blood with a side of intestines rained down on the hangar floor.

Sabio raced through the thick smoke, desperately searching for his partner amid the bloody mess. "Desmond," he cried out.

Sabio heard a moan. He saw movement from a heap of green mangled flesh and brain matter. He offered his hand, which the pulping mass of flesh and goo used to get back to his feet. Sabio then tackled the goo into a hug.

"I'm good. I'm good," Desmond said, spitting out blood and brain bits from his mouth. "You good?"

"I'm good," Sabio reassured him, and let go. "But my undies aren't."

They laughed and then looked at what remained of Dorkhovich. It's as if they had just entered the world's largest meat market. There was blood and raw meat everywhere.

Silver Fox limped her way toward the men, massaging her head from the fall.

"You all right?" Desmond asked.

Silver Fox nodded. "How did you survive the explosion?"

The Superspy said nothing. An explosion of that type should have killed him along with Dorkhovich. Yet, somehow, he knew it wouldn't.

"It doesn't matter," Sabio interrupted. "He's alive. You're alive, and I'm alive. We did it. Mission accomplished!" He put his arm around the pair and shook his hips into song and dance.

While Sabio busied himself with his dancing moves, the two veteran agents shared the same look of concern. They understood that Dorkhovich was just one of who knew how many. The Black Hand had finally revealed itself after so many years, and it was an impressive introduction.

This was only the beginning. The Black Hand was cracking its knuckles.

Chapter 20

Aliana May

Desmond pulled into the underground parking structure of his apartment complex. He turned off the engine once he parked at his stall and checked the rearview mirror to make sure his tie was on straight. It was. He then hurried out of his car, wearing a blue business suit, with a black leather briefcase wedged in between his armpit, before stopping two steps short of the elevator doors. He sighed, hurried back to his car, and opened the passenger-side door to pull out the bouquet of roses he got for Aliana.

Easy, Desmond, easy.

He took a deep breath, and calmly made his way back to the elevator. As he waited for the thirty-first floor to ding, he was not convinced that things would go smoothly this time. No explanation he could think of was good enough to forgive his four-day disappearing act. Roses was a good way to start. Hopefully, she would notice them over the half-dozen bandages stickered all over his face.

"Aliana," he called out, closing the door behind him. "You home?" he asked but was met with silence.

Desmond walked into the kitchen and to his surprise found it a complete mess. The sink was full of dirty dishes. The stove was covered in layers of grease. Unopened mail lay scattered atop the kitchen table with a few envelopes lying on the tile floor that was in desperate need of a mop.

"Babe?" he walked into the bedroom. "You in here?"

The bedroom was no different than the kitchen. The bed was unmade, covers thrown on the ground, and the laundry basket rested in the corner of the room with clothes piled on top of each other.

This wasn't like her. Aliana was a neat freak. The fact that the place was a mess meant that something was seriously wrong.

"I'm sorry, Mr. Williams, but Aliana has requested a personal leave of absence," the receptionist informed Desmond over the phone. "She hasn't been to work since her vacation."

"All right. Thank you," Desmond hung up. So much for a surprise luncheon.

Where could she be?

Desmond left the apartment and toured the city, not realizing he was still carrying the bouquet of roses. His four day mission across the scenic continent had made him forgot how loud and busy everything was back home. The metropolis was buzzing with such high frequency energy that it hurt Desmond's eyes, and ear. But Aliana had insisted on living in the middle of it all to suit her lifestyle and needs. Unfortunately for Desmond, the city was a good two-hour drive from the nearest Agency base. The commute was bearable, but not worth it. Had the drive been from the suburbs then he would have nothing to complain about.

Desmond loved the suburbs. Suburbia was where his heart was. Life was on a different plane in the outskirts of town: white picket fences, two-story houses, quiet neighborhoods, trees, weekend BBQs, and friendly neighbors who looked after each other. The peaceful setting was a far cry from the buzzing sounds the city was known for. It seemed to slow down time so you could enjoy it all. Maybe it was time to move away. Maybe it was time to leave it all behind and start something new in a two-story house.

He would need to find Aliana first before making that decision.

"Have you seen Aliana?" Desmond asked the waitress at the local bakery. The staff had grown accustomed to seeing the two love birds every morning. Their a.m. ritual consisted of a hot cup of coffee with a Danish bun. If anyone had seen Aliana it would have to be the bakery.

"Uh..." the waitress paused. "Nope. Haven't seen her in a while. Come to think of it, haven't seen either of you in a while. Thought you two were dead."

"Vacation. Same thing. Thanks."

"You bet. Nice suit."

Desmond smirked, not realizing he was still wearing his flashy attire.

Desmond drove through the city for hours, not sure where to look next. After a while he was tempted to put a call to the Agency. Sabio could easily work his magic and find her in a matter of minutes. Desmond dismissed the thought. This was a personal matter. Not theirs. It was Desmond Williams, and not the Superspy, looking for his missing girlfriend.

After another hour of aimless driving, his instinctive nature kicked in, and his car revved onto the onramp towards Highway 101. Four-hours later, he arrived at the Bookstore thirty minutes before closing.

Desmond made his way inside and walked past the book aisles and display tables, stopping at the café, where he found a woman sitting by her lonesome at the corner table.

Aliana?

He couldn't tell. Her hair was tied back into a bun with loose strands hanging off to the side. She wore a wrinkled blue dress shirt with black leggings and sneakers. She was a mess. Not Aliana's style. Aliana was all about looking good all the time, even in casual attire.

As if the woman knew she was being watched, she looked directly at Desmond, and that's when he saw the bags underneath her green eyes. It *was* Aliana.

Desmond smiled and waved. She turned away, and refused to look at him, even when he sat across from her. Even with all the bandages stuck to his face. Neither spoke a word. They watched people come and go in silence.

"The hour is now nine thirty p.m. We will be closing in ten minutes," the intercom announced. "Please make your final selections. We thank you for shopping at the Bookstore."

Aliana scooped up her belongings and pushed her chair back against the table before walking out. Desmond followed closely behind. They walked across the parking lot until they arrived at her car. Aliana dropped her car keys when she reached inside her purse.

Desmond quickly knelt down and picked them up. He handed them back to her; she took them without a single word, and unlocked the driver-side door.

Desmond broke the silence. "Aliana, talk to me."

She paused.

"I'm sorry," he said softly.

"You left me," she spoke sadly, her eyes on the ground.

"I know I did."

"You left me alone. I had no idea where you went. I was worried." She looked up at him with watery eyes. "Why would you do that to me?"

"Because—"

"Because...*why?*" She focused on Desmond's eyes, pleading for an answer. One that would make the hurt go away.

"Because sometimes...I just don't think."

I think about you all the time.

"And...I'll do stupid things that probably don't make sense."

To protect you. The one I love. The one I truly love.

"But you're always in my thoughts."

No matter where I go. I do it all for you.

"But you left me on our two-year anniversary. You left me like you always do...to go do something that could have waited another day."

"You're right. You're absolutely right. I left you to take care of something that you couldn't possibly understand, and...I can't take back what I did. I can only learn from it. I'm sorry."

Aliana was quiet.

"I promise not to leave you again," Desmond said, knowing that such a promise was impossible in his line of work. "I love you," he said out loud. "I've loved you since the first day we met. And you annoyed me that day. You were a real pain in my ass." He laughed.

Aliana half smiled.

"You were such a dork," he continued. "The biggest dork I've ever met."

"You're a bigger dork," she said, smiling.

Desmond cupped her hands into his own. He pulled her in close, and the two looked closely at each other. "What I love about you is..."

Aliana burst into laughter.

"What? Thought I'd forgot, didn't you?"

"That was *sooooooo* four days ago."

"True. But I didn't forget." Desmond cleared his throat. "What I love about you is...that you're understanding, compassionate, funny, warm on those cold nights—"

Aliana laughed.

"I love the fact that you enjoy cereal and pizza as much as I do, and no matter how stupid I get, you'll always find room in your heart to forgive me."

"Cheater," she blurted it out.

"I can't see myself with anyone else but you. You're my everything."

The two lovebirds hugged, then kissed passionately. When their lips came undone, Desmond looked at his girlfriend and spoke those words that Aliana had been waiting to hear for the past five days.

"Happy anniversary," he whispered.

"Happy anniversary," she whispered back.

Epilogue

Mark Stencil sat his butt down comfortably against the cushion of a luxurious leather chair. Spotlights lay overhead, illuminating the bureau chief as though he were about to perform on stage. Before him sat the mysterious governing body of Agency High Command, backlit by blue glowing lights that gave the group the ethereal glow they were said to have. Everything else was covered in shadow.

Mark had been summoned to give a full report on the four-day operation the governing body had labeled, "The Great Feast."

"The Superspy?" one of them asked, his voice echoing from the boundaries of empty space.

"Deactivated for now. But aware of the upcoming threat."

"What of Roberto Gonzalez?"

"Roberto Gonzalez was buried in his family plot in Mexico. His surviving wife and daughter are currently under the care of the

Agency and have been placed in protective custody in case the Black Hand tries to kidnap them."

"Your men couldn't save Roberto. What makes you think you can save the mother and daughter?"

"We can at least try to keep them safe."

"What of this mysterious plant—*chile sangre?*" a different voice called out.

"Our scientists have confiscated the seeds and are currently running tests on them to isolate the chemical known to cause the flesh-eating sickness. It turns out Roberto Gonzalez had a secret field in Mexico where he was growing the plant. That's how he was able to continue mass production on his Agua Dulce sauce. The seeds in his heart were a necessity in case something happened to those fields. Or to him. Upon his death, the seeds were meant to be passed on to the company's next heir, his daughter. Without the plant, I doubt the Gato Negro empire will remain functional. I hear production has declined."

"What of Dorkhovich?" a third voice asked.

"The remains of his body have been studied and dissected."

"And?" the fourth and final voice beckoned.

"And we have isolated a mysterious green substance in his spinal fluid." Stencil became serious. He shifted his weight on the chair. "It's the same substance that was found in Billy Bob Billy Jeff Jenkins's and TJBJ's blood. We believe it gives them their extraordinary abilities."

"Then why weren't the brothers enlarged like Dorkhovich?"

"That I'm not sure of. We have no idea what it is or how it works. Only that it grants immeasurable power. And that horrifies us."

"Why?"

"Because Dorkhovich was only a demonstration. Who knows how many elite soldiers are out there, pumped full of this substance. More powerful and dangerous than Dorkhovich."

"What came of the mysterious woman who cared for the Russian?"

"Her whereabouts are unknown at this time," Stencil confessed.

"And of the Black Hand? Any success?"

"No."

"But you've got Billy Bob Billy Jeff Jenkins in custody. He must know something."

"He doesn't. He spoke to the Black Hand only once, and that was after his breakout from Black Portal."

There was a deep sigh in the room. Stencil could feel the air of disappointment coming from the four mysterious figures.

"Anything else you'd like to report?" one voice asked.

"Yes. A couple of days ago, a computer programmer came to our doorstep. To our physical doorstep at Agency Command."

"How is that possible? Agency Command is unknown. Even to us."

"He had no trouble finding it. Even knew who I was. Says he needs our help. That the Black Hand is trying to recruit him through persuasive methods."

"Such as?"

"His girlfriend. She's been kidnapped. He needs our help to get her back. I consider him a valuable asset…but also a threat."

"Why?"

"If he joins us, then he could lead us to the location of the Black Hand. But if he joins them, I'm sure he'll lead the Black Hand to our doorstep. Maybe even to yours."

The governing body muttered to themselves in whispers. After a minute, they came to a conclusion.

"We consider this matter urgent. Reactivate Agent Darby…and the Superspy."

Acknowledgments

I'd like to thank my wife, Ermelinda (whose name nobody knows how to pronounce correctly), for putting up with me every weekend for months on end. Thank you for letting me stay home on the weekends to work on this book when I knew you wanted to go out and enjoy the day. Thanks to my dad, who continues to encourage me to pursue my dreams. Thank you for always being proud of me for every accomplishment I have been able to achieve; no matter how small or unimportant others may have thought it was, you were always proud. I couldn't have finished this book without your love and support. Love you both.

And of course, thank you, dear reader, for taking the time and, most notably, *money* to purchase this book. I hope you enjoyed reading it as much as I had fun rewriting it over and over and over and over and over and over again.

See you next time!

About the Author

Eddie Ayala is an avid writer and reader who enjoys telling stories. He holds degrees in humanities and languages, and radio, TV, and film. He currently resides in Fontana, California, with his wife, Ermelinda, and dogs, Zoe and Blanca; he hopes to one day become an accomplished author.

www.ingramcontent.com/pod-product-compliance
Lightning Source LLC
Chambersburg PA
CBHW070804180626
46818CB00001B/99